J
D

The Mark of the Blue Tattoo

As the Freddy Frost truck picked up speed, Joe groped desperately for a handhold. He saw a narrow gap between the top of the rear door and the truck body. He wedged his fingertips into it— just in time. With a lurch, the truck crashed through the gate.

At the next rough movement, Joe knew he'd be thrown to the pavement. He had to find a better grip, but where? He craned his neck and saw the frame that encircled the roof and held the Freddy Frost lights and sign. How solid was the frame? he wondered. He knew he had no choice—the only way to find out was to try it.

Tightening his left hand into a claw to strengthen his hold on the top of the door, Joe let go with his right hand and reached up as far as he could. He felt his feet leave the bumper. He crouched slightly, willed all the power into his legs, then leaped. He shut his eyes, sure he was about to crash to the street. . . .

The Hardy Boys
Mystery Stories

Available from MINSTREL Books

THE HARDY BOYS®

146

THE MARK OF THE BLUE TATTOO

FRANKLIN W. DIXON

A MINSTREL® BOOK

Published by POCKET BOOKS
New York   London   Toronto   Sydney   Tokyo   Singapore

This book is a work of fiction. Names, characters, places and incidents are products of the author's imagination or are used fictitiously. Any resemblance to actual events or locales or persons, living or dead, is entirely coincidental.

A MINSTREL PAPERBACK *Original*

A Minstrel Book published by
POCKET BOOKS, a division of Simon & Schuster Inc.
1230 Avenue of the Americas, New York, NY 10020

Copyright © 1997 by Simon & Schuster Inc.

Front cover illustration by John Youssi

Produced by Mega-Books, Inc.

ISBN: 0-671-00058-6

First Minstrel Books printing October 1997

10 9 8 7 6 5 4 3 2 1

THE HARDY BOYS MYSTERY STORIES is a trademark of Simon & Schuster Inc.

THE HARDY BOYS, A MINSTREL BOOK and colophon are registered trademarks of Simon & Schuster Inc.

Printed in the U.S.A.

Contents

THE MARK OF THE
BLUE TATTOO

1 A Call for Help

Joe Hardy carried his lunch tray across the crowded cafeteria of Bayport High School. Tall and blond, he moved with the casual grace of a star running back. Two girls, deep in conversation, crossed directly in front of him. Without breaking stride, Joe neatly stepped around them without spilling a drop of his soda.

Joe's older brother, Frank, was already at the table where they usually sat, against the far wall. Frank was sitting with his girlfriend, Callie Shaw. They were listening closely to their friend Chet Morton. As Joe approached, they looked up and smiled. Joe put his tray down next to Chet's.

"Joe, wait until you hear this," Chet said. "I

just had this incredibly brilliant idea. How does guacamole sherbet sound?"

"Yuck!" Joe said, making a face. "Are you guys having a gross-out contest or what?"

"Chet's new job starts this afternoon," Frank explained. "He's going to be driving a Freddy Frost ice-cream truck."

"The company's having a contest," Chet added.

"The person who comes up with the best idea for a new flavor before the end of the week gets a free ice cream every day for a year. I'm not eligible because I work for Freddy Frost, but I want to show them how enthusiastic I am."

"Guacamole sherbet?" Joe repeated in disbelief. "Would you serve it in a cone made out of corn chips?"

Chet's jaw dropped. "That's it, Joe! I knew I needed a gimmick that would grab people, and you just gave it to me. Maybe they'll put my picture on the wrapper."

"They will," Callie said with a laugh, "with 'Wanted' under it."

"Genius is always misunderstood," Chet said with a hurt expression. "It's the penalty for being ahead of my time."

"You just gave me an idea, though," Callie added. "I'll bet cream cheese and jelly ice cream would be terrific."

"Not you, too!" Joe groaned. He looked up and

2

spotted his girlfriend, Iola Morton, coming toward them. He smiled and waved.

Iola was Chet's sister. She put her tray next to Joe's and sat down. "Has Chet been telling you about his new dessert inventions?" she asked.

Frank chuckled. "He certainly has."

A grin spread across Iola's face. "Did he mention last night?" she continued. "He was in the kitchen for hours working on a secret formula for—get this—cheeseburger ice cream."

"That reminds me," Joe said. "I forgot to get ketchup." He pushed his chair back. As he was getting to his feet, another student bumped into him and gave the leg of his chair a sharp kick.

"Hey, watch it," Joe said over his shoulder.

"No, *you* watch it, turkey."

Joe turned to face his opponent, who was an inch or so under six feet tall, with broad shoulders and a bull neck. His dark hair was cropped close at the sides and back, and left long on top. He was wearing baggy jeans, unlaced work boots, and a black T-shirt with the image of a heavy metal group on the front.

"I'm afraid you blew your line," Joe said with a tight smile. "When you crash into somebody, you're supposed to say, 'sorry.'"

Joe drew himself up. There was a flicker of indecision in his opponent's eyes as he realized that Joe outreached and outweighed him.

3

"Joe, let it go," Iola said, taking his elbow. "It's not worth the hassle."

With a shrug, Joe took a half step backward. The boy sneered and walked away.

Joe looked over at his friends. "Who's Mr. Attitude?" he asked. "Anybody know him?"

"I do," Callie replied. "That's Gus French. He's in my history class. He's pretty tight with Marlon Masters."

There was a short silence. Marlon Masters was the most powerful gang leader at Bayport High. Joe and Frank had never tangled with him and his followers—yet, at least.

"So, he's one of the Starz, right?" Joe said, using the gang name that had recently started appearing on walls and desktops around school. "I wonder if he bumped me by accident or if he was trying to start something."

"Accident," Frank said. "Bet on it. If he'd done it on purpose, he would have brought a few buddies along as backup."

Joe noticed Mr. Vincenza, the school counselor, striding across the cafeteria. He stopped next to their table and said, "Joe, Frank? Could I speak to you for a second?"

The Hardys followed Mr. Vincenza out into the corridor. Joe wondered if they were in some kind of trouble.

"Boys, I need your help," Mr. Vincenza began, after glancing around. "There's an epidemic

4

starting at Bayport High. We've got to get it under control, before it's too late."

"What is it?" Joe asked. "Flu?"

"No. Something a lot more serious than that. Extortion," Mr. Vincenza replied. "Our younger students are being forced to make payoffs to avoid being assaulted. That's bad enough at any time. But the town council is going to be taking up a plan to help the high school. If this gets into the papers, it could badly damage us for years to come."

"What can we do?" Frank asked.

"Everybody knows that you're both skilled detectives," Mr. Vincenza said. "And you have the advantage of being students yourselves. What I want you to do is find out who is behind all this. Give us the evidence we need to stop them."

"We'll do our best," Joe promised.

"I knew I could count on you," Mr. Vincenza said. He took a card from his pocket and wrote on the back. "Here are my office and home numbers. If you need to reach me, call."

Joe and Frank returned to their friends in the cafeteria. As they sat down, Chet said, "Hey, guys. What about pizza sherbet? How does that grab you?"

Joe clutched his stomach. "It grabs me," he said. "Right about here. And I can tell you, it's not a pleasant feeling."

* * *

After school Joe and Frank met near the parking lot.

"Any luck?" Frank asked.

"Some people in my classes have heard about kids getting leaned on for money," Joe replied. "I got the names of a couple of victims, both freshmen. We can call them later. How about you—did you find out anything?"

Frank shook his head. "I tried to get more information about the Starz, but nobody wanted to talk about them. We can try again tomorrow. For now, why don't we go find Callie and Iola? I want to surprise Chet by waiting for him somewhere along his ice-cream route."

"Great idea," Joe said with a chuckle. "As long as you don't expect me to try one of his specials. But how do we find out his route?"

"Iola might know," Frank said. "If she doesn't, we could call the Freddy Frost office. As detective work goes, it should be something we can handle without Dad's help," he added with a sly grin.

Joe grinned back. Their father, Fenton Hardy, had held a high post in the New York City Police Department before retiring to become a private investigator.

Callie and Iola came into view. Frank waved them over, then told them his idea.

"Perfect," Iola said. "I have to go home first,

but we can catch Chet next to the playground in Jefferson Park at around four-thirty."

"Good deal," Joe said, grinning. "I'll even order one of his special broccoli sundaes."

"Is that the one with a brussels sprout on top of the whipped cream, instead of a cherry?" Frank asked with an innocent look.

"I'd better go," Iola said, "before I throw up. See you later."

After Iola headed home, Joe, Frank, and Callie took the Hardy's van to Mr. Pizza for a snack. Then they drove across town to Jefferson Park. The park took up two square blocks in one of the older sections of Bayport. Around the park stood rows of narrow two-story houses, each with its own front yard and covered porch.

Iola was waiting for them on a bench next to the playground. "Am I glad to see you," she said. "I looked at Chet's schedule when I got home. He was due here earlier than I thought. I was afraid you'd miss him."

Joe listened for a moment. He could hear the shouts of kids in the playground and the hum of traffic over on Winthrop Street. He even heard the rustle of leaves from nearby trees—but not the tinkly sounds of the Freddy Frost music.

"He can't be that close, or we'd hear the theme song," Joe said.

Callie started humming the tune. Joe sang

7

along. The tune was that of a nursery rhyme. But anyone who had grown up in Bayport knew a different set of words:

> Freddy Frost is such a treat
> We bring dessert right to your street
> For frozen yogurt or soft ice cream
> Get Freddy Frost today!

"*Ice cream* doesn't rhyme with *today*," Frank pointed out.

"You're right. I never noticed that when we were growing up," Iola replied. "Who cares? What I want to know is, where's Chet? I can't believe he'd get lost on his first day."

"Maybe he's selling so much stuff that he fell behind schedule," Joe suggested. "Let's go back along his route and look for him instead of just sitting here."

The others agreed that this was a good idea and piled into the van.

"Go back along Jefferson and turn right on Cuyler Street," Iola told Joe. "There's a school playground a couple of blocks up."

As he pulled away from the curb, Joe checked his side mirror. A few cars back, he noticed a red compact with a badly dented front fender starting to pull out of its parking place. Joe made sure his turn signal was on, then followed Iola's directions.

8

At the playground they found ten or fifteen children, but no Freddy Frost truck. Joe was about to ask Iola for more of Chet's route. Then he noticed something. One little girl in the playground was on the last bites of an ice-cream bar.

"Wait here a sec," Joe told his friends. "I think we just missed Chet." He climbed out and went over to the closest trash basket. Near the top were two torn Freddy Frost wrappers. So, unless there was more than one truck assigned to this route, Chet *had* been here.

Two boys playing tag came running toward him. "Hey," Joe called. "Did you guys see an ice-cream truck?"

The boy in front stopped. "Sure," he said. "A little while ago. I wanted to get a Rainbow Rocket, but the man didn't wait. He just drove away. I don't get it."

"Maybe he didn't see you coming," Joe said.

"Maybe," the boy said doubtfully.

"He saw us. It was those two other guys who made him hurry," the second boy said. "They got in the truck with him, and then he drove off."

Joe frowned. "Two other guys? Who were they? What did they look like?"

The second boy shrugged. "I don't know. They both had ski masks over their faces. That was pretty weird. It's not cold out."

"Yeah," the first boy said. "And those two guys kept shoving the Freddy Frost man like they didn't like him."

Joe froze. Chet driving away with two men wearing ski masks could only mean one thing—he'd been kidnapped!

2 Kidnapped!

"That does sound weird," Joe said to the two boys, trying to sound as calm as possible. He asked them a few more questions about the two men. How tall were they? What else were they wearing? Had they come in a car? Was anyone else with them? It was no use; the ski masks were all that had stuck in the boys' minds—that and missing out on getting Freddy Frost ice cream.

Joe got their names and thanked them. Then he hurried back to the van. He told the others what he had just found out.

"They must be kidnappers!" Iola exclaimed. "But why Chet? And what are we going to do?"

11

"Maybe it wasn't Chet they were after. Maybe they wanted the money in the truck," Callie suggested. "Chet might have had several hundred dollars on him."

"I can think of another possibility, too," Frank said. "Remember, this *is* Chet's first day. Maybe the hijacking is a fake, some kind of hazing that the other drivers put new people through."

"You mean, a practical joke?" Iola asked. "That is so mean. Chet must be incredibly upset."

"We won't know until we find him," Joe pointed out. "And I'm sure we can find him. A Freddy Frost truck is pretty conspicuous."

"So are a couple of guys in ski masks," Frank pointed out.

Joe nodded. "Right. So whatever those guys were after, whether it was ice cream or money or some weird fun, my hunch is that they didn't go far. I say we start searching the neighborhood right around here."

As he said this, Joe glanced in his rearview mirror. The red car with the crumpled fender was parked at the curb about fifty feet back. Joe could see the silhouette of a driver at the wheel.

"Frank," Joe said. "I think we've grown a tail. Red, three cars back. Let's get a look at him."

"Right," Frank replied, reaching for his door handle. "Ready?"

Joe and Frank opened their doors at the same moment and stepped out of the van. Joe walked along the street side of the parked cars, while Frank took the sidewalk.

They hadn't taken more than a dozen steps before Joe heard an engine roar into life. The red car shot out of its space, made a quick U-turn, and sped away.

Joe ran to join Frank on the sidewalk. "Did you get a look at him?" he asked.

"I got a good look at his sunglasses," Frank said with a rueful expression. "Very large. Very dark. How about you?"

"The rear license plate was pretty muddy, but I made out *P*-something-something, then three-seven-two," Joe replied. "When we get home, we can use Dad's password to access the Motor Vehicles database. With luck, we'll be able to narrow it down to a few possibilities."

The brothers turned to walk back to the van. "When did you first notice that guy?" Frank asked.

"When we drove away from Jefferson Park," Joe told him. "Interesting . . . he must have followed us there from school. Why, I wonder."

"There's something else, too," Frank said. "If he was busy following us, he couldn't have been wearing a ski mask and abducting Chet at the same time. So that means—"

"He could be in cahoots with the ski masks," Joe finished for his brother. "What that means is the whole thing was planned ahead of time *and* by someone who knows we're friends of Chet's. They even guessed we might decide to meet him somewhere along the route."

"What was *that* all about?" Callie asked as Frank and Joe climbed back into the van.

Frank recapped the conversation he and Joe had just had.

"I just know that Chet is in some awful danger," Iola said. "Can't we do anything?"

As Joe started the engine, he said, "Sure. We can look for him. You watch the left side, and Frank and Callie will watch the right side. Call out if you see anything even a little bit suspicious."

Joe turned onto the first street leading away from the playground, then drove slowly for five blocks until he reached the next major cross street. There he turned right, then right again at the next corner, and he followed that street back to the playground. As he drove, Frank, Iola, and Callie scanned the driveways and what they could see of the backyards. They saw cars, vans, and campers—but nothing that looked even remotely like a Freddy Frost truck.

After half an hour of slow cruising, Iola let out

an exasperated sigh. "This isn't going to work," she declared. "And while we're wasting our time like this, my brother's in danger."

Joe stopped at the curb and turned to look at Iola. Her face was pale, and her lips were red where she'd been biting them. He reached back and patted her hand. "Don't worry," he said. "We're on the case. We'll do everything we can to find him."

"What if that's not enough?" Iola cried. "I think we should call the police."

Frank shook his head. "And tell them what? That the ice-cream truck didn't show up at Jefferson Park this afternoon?" he asked. "They'd laugh at us. For all we know, Chet simply decided to change his route. He may even be back at the Freddy Frost plant by now."

"What about the two guys in ski masks?" Iola replied angrily. "Did those kids imagine them?"

Frank nodded. "It's possible. And it's possible that they were taking part in a practical joke. I'll bet that's what the cops would think. It's a matter of odds. A lot more people have pranks played on them than get kidnapped."

"Look," Joe said. "We've done practically every street in a five-block radius around the playground. I say we finish the search of this area before we decide to try some other method. How does that sound, Iola?"

15

Iola looked torn, but finally she nodded.

Joe pulled the van away from the curb and started down the street again. Toward the end of the block he noticed a house on the left. The paint was peeling, and weeds grew high in the yard. Near the sidewalk, a faded For Sale sign drooped backward. The house was obviously empty.

Joe slowed the van down to a crawl. "Look!" he exclaimed, hitting the brakes. "There's a fresh tire track in the dirt next to the driveway, and the weeds have been crushed down. That's got to mean something!"

He jumped out of the van and dashed across the street with Frank, Callie, and Iola close behind. Behind the house was a garage. One of the doors sagged partly open. Joe ran over and peered through the opening. "Over here!" he called. "Hurry!"

Inside the garage Joe saw the familiar shape of a Freddy Frost truck. Joe grabbed the edge of the door and tugged it open. Frank pulled at the other door.

Iola rushed in. A moment later, she called, "Chet's over here! He's tied up!"

Joe and the others hurried over. Chet was sitting on the garage floor. His wrists and ankles were fastened with heavy gray tape. Another strip of tape covered his mouth.

16

"Mmm-m-m," Chet said, giving them a pleading look.

Frank held one side of the tape across Chet's mouth. "This is going to hurt," he warned. He peeled off the tape with a snap of his wrist.

"Ouch!" Chet exclaimed, rubbing his cheek. "You weren't kidding!"

Meanwhile, Joe was using the scissors blade on his pocketknife to cut through the tape on Chet's wrists and ankles. When he finished, he and Iola helped Chet to his feet.

"Thanks, guys. I thought I might have to spend the rest of my life in here," Chet said, wobbling a little.

"What happened?" Iola asked.

"I was parked at a playground, selling a little girl a Freddy Fudgie, when I heard the door of the truck slide open," Chet told them. "I turned around and saw these two guys wearing ski masks. They told me to get moving or else."

"Were they armed?" Frank asked.

Chet shrugged. "I don't know for sure. They said they were, and they kept putting their hands in their pockets. I didn't feel like finding out. Anyway, they told me to drive here. One of them opened the garage. Once we were inside, they tied me up and left."

17

"Just like that?" Joe asked. "What about your money?"

"It's still in my belt pouch," Chet replied. "They weren't interested in the money. They didn't even help themselves to a free ice cream. It's weird, I know. But that's what happened. Maybe they just don't like me."

"I wonder if any of the other Freddy Frost drivers have had this kind of harassment," Frank said.

"I can ask around," Chet said. "Not that I really know anybody yet. Why? What do you think it means?"

"This could be part of a plot to extort money from the company," Frank said. "You know— 'Pay us off, or we'll ruin your business.'"

"That would mean that they weren't after Chet personally," Iola pointed out. "I'd like that a lot better."

Chet broke into a grin. "Believe me, so would I. But listen, guys, I'd better get back to selling some ice cream. I don't get paid for lying around in a garage with tape on my face."

"Just one thing," Joe said. "You said you heard the truck door slide open. Wouldn't the truck door have been locked?"

A look of surprise crossed Chet's face. "Yeah . . . I mean I thought it was. Company rules—keep the truck locked at all times. I guess I must have messed up."

"Maybe," Joe said. "Or maybe the guys who got in had a key."

"An inside job, you mean?" Callie asked.

"It makes sense in a way," Joe told her. "The crooks knew where to find Chet. And they'd obviously decided to use this garage in advance."

"There's one thing I should tell you," Chet said reluctantly, staring at the floor. "Both of those guys were wearing gloves. But when they were taping me up, I got a glimpse of one guy's wrist. He had a tattoo there. A little blue star."

Joe frowned, as he tried to figure out what this implied. "The Starz?" he finally said. "Do they have tattoos? Do you think—"

"I don't know," Chet replied. He sounded tired all of a sudden. "Lots of people have tattoos. Maybe it doesn't mean anything at all."

"It's quite a coincidence, though," Frank said. "We just had problems with the Starz at lunchtime. Mr. Vincenza asks us to look into a problem that sounds gang-related. And a few hours later, you get harassed. I'd say we need to take a very close look at Marlon and his buddies."

"I'm glad you're okay," Iola said, taking her brother's arm. "What would have happened if we hadn't come looking for you? Would those guys have left you here to starve?"

Chet turned pale at the thought. He was

opening his mouth to reply, when one of the garage doors was flung back with a crash.

"Freeze!" a voice shouted. A powerful flashlight beam flooded the inside of the garage. Narrowing his eyes against the glare, Joe saw the outlines of two people crouched in the opening. Both of them were holding guns.

3 Tracking the Tailer

"Freeze!" the voice yelled again. "Police!"

Frank stood still, his hands held carefully away from his sides. He knew that the two police officers had no way of knowing what they would face inside the gloomy garage, and he didn't want to do anything that might make them nervous. Moments later he and his friends were braced against the wall of the garage with their hands over their heads and their feet spread wide.

"Hey, wait a minute, Anderson," one of the officers said, as his partner, a woman, started to frisk Callie. "Those two over there are Fenton Hardy's kids. You know, the private eye. They're okay."

Frank recognized the voice of Officer Con Riley. Frank and Joe had helped Riley on several of his cases. As a result, he was one of the few members of the Bayport Police Force who treated the Hardy brothers as useful resources instead of nuisances.

After telling Frank and his friends to straighten up, Riley asked, "And what might you be doing on private property with an ice-cream truck?"

Chet quickly explained.

"Two guys in ski masks?" Officer Anderson repeated skeptically. "That sounds like something you got out of a movie."

"Yeah, a horror movie," Chet replied. "But no, this was real."

As Frank had predicted to his friends earlier, Riley said, "But they didn't take anything—money, merchandise, right? Sounds like a practical joke that went too far. Do you know anybody who has a grudge against you, son?" he asked Chet.

Chet shook his head, then glanced at Frank, as if to ask if he should mention the Starz. Frank in turn gave a tiny shake of his head. One briefly glimpsed tattoo wasn't enough evidence to accuse Marlon's gang of being criminals, he thought.

Before the police officers could pose any more questions, Frank asked, "What brought you here?"

"We got a phone call," Riley said. "Suspicious activity. Prowler."

"Was it an anonymous call?" Joe asked eagerly.

"That's right," Riley said.

"Did the caller mention us?" Callie asked. "I mean, did he say a bunch of people? Or just a prowler?"

Riley hesitated, then said, "I'd have to check the taped record of the call. But to the best of my recollection, he said 'a prowler breaking into the garage.'"

"I'll bet it was the kidnappers!" Iola exclaimed. "They wanted to make sure that Chet was found. That makes me feel a lot better."

"Not me," Chet retorted, rubbing the red marks left on his wrists by the tape. "Iola, thinking that the kidnappers were concerned for my welfare sounds like wishful thinking to me. Personally, I'd like to string them up by their thumbs."

He glanced at his watch and added, "If I don't put in some more time on my route, this is going to be my first and last day on the job. Is that okay, officers?"

Anderson closed her notebook and said, "Fine. We've got your phone numbers, in case we have any more questions." Reaching for her coin purse, she added, "By the way, do you guys still carry Freddy Fudgies? That used to be a favorite of mine. I haven't had one in years."

Chet climbed into the truck and found a Freddy Fudgie for Officer Anderson. Then the officers left. While Frank and Joe held the sagging garage doors open, Callie and Iola guided Chet as he drove backward down the driveway and onto the street. Moments later the melody of "Freddy Frost is such a treat" tinkled through the neighborhood again.

As she got into the van, Iola said, "Do you think we could follow him? It'll make him feel better, and I'd like to be sure nothing else happens to him today."

"That sounds like a good idea," Frank said. He glanced at his wristwatch. "It's already after six. He'll have to take the truck back pretty soon."

Joe started the van and began to creep down the street in the wake of the Freddy Frost truck. At his second stop, Chet leaned out the window and waved to them. Then he gestured for them to go ahead. Apparently he had regained his confidence.

"What now? Call it a day?" Joe asked.

Frank glanced back at Callie and Iola. As he did, he noticed a familiar red compact car halfway down the block. It was double-parked in front of a convenience store.

"Joe, our tail's back," Frank said. "Make a quick U-turn, and let's see if we can get a good look at him."

Even before Frank finished his sentence, Joe

24

cranked the wheel over and hit the gas. The rear end of the van fishtailed, then straightened out.

As they barreled down the street toward the red car, Joe switched on the headlights, on high beam. Frank got a solid look at the car's driver before he, in turn, floored his accelerator and roared away, tires squealing.

"Male, white, about thirty-five," Frank said aloud. "Round face, balding, gold stud in left earlobe."

Joe added, "Wearing designer sunglasses and a red-and-green Hawaiian shirt. And the missing letters on the license plate are *T* and *M.*"

"You guys are amazing," Callie said with admiration. "I only got about half of that."

"Early training," Frank explained. "Dad used to play Kim's Game with us when we were little."

"What's that?" asked Iola.

"It's from a book by Kipling," Joe replied. "The way the hero, Kim, learned to be observant was, they'd show him a tray with a couple of dozen gemstones on it for a minute or so. Then they'd cover it, and he'd have to name as many as he could—from memory."

"Dad didn't use gemstones, though," Frank added. "He used all kinds of other stuff— stamps, paper clips, matchbooks, ballpoint pens. It was fun."

"Especially when we finally started getting everything right," Joe said with a laugh. "Until then, I thought it was the pits. Uh-oh," he said, looking at his watch. "We'd better be getting home."

Callie was planning to give Iola a ride home, but her car was still at school. Joe drove to the parking lot. As the girls were getting out, Joe said, "Iola, will you tell Chet that we'll drop by to see him after dinner?"

Iola smiled. "Are you planning to grill him?" she asked, teasing.

"Just a few routine questions, ma'am," Joe replied.

More seriously, Frank said, "At the start of a case, you never know what information might give you the clue you need to solve it."

"By the way," Callie said, "Iola and I were in at the beginning, and we plan to stay in until we solve this case. Right, Iola?"

"Of course," Iola said emphatically. "And don't forget about Chet himself. You'll hurt his feelings if you don't let him help."

"We'll remember that," Frank promised.

When Frank and Joe reached home, they booted their computer and logged on to the Net. Ten minutes later, they had traced the license-plate number they needed. The red compact car belonged to a car-rental agency in Martin's Landing, a town about twenty miles from Bayport.

Joe looked at Frank. "Looks like we'll have to

find out who our tail is the old-fashioned way—by asking him."

"And hope we can keep him in one place long enough for us to find out the answer," Frank added with a grin.

After dinner the Hardys drove over to the Morton house. Chet met them at the door. "Come on back to the family room," he said. "Iola's upstairs doing homework. I just made some popcorn."

Joe sniffed the air. "With extra butter," he said. "It smells great."

The three friends settled around the table in the family room with the bowl of popcorn in the middle.

"What kind of reception did you get when you went back to Freddy Frost?" Joe asked Chet.

"Pretty normal, I guess," Chet replied. "Nobody showed any sign of knowing what had happened. No funny looks, no snickers, nothing."

"Did you tell anybody what happened?" Joe asked. "How did they respond?"

"I had to tell Sal," Chet replied. "Sal Vitello, he's my supervisor. It's funny. At first he was pretty nice about everything. When I came in late, he said not to worry about it. But then, after he heard my story, he turned cold. Maybe he thought I was making up the whole thing as an excuse."

"What about the other drivers? Have you gotten to know any of them yet?" Frank asked.

Chet frowned. "I've seen most of them and met a few," he said. "A lot of us are new, you know—not just me. A lot of the Freddy Frost people work just over the summer. Then around September, when the ice-cream season is ending, they have to fill in with new people. There are some familiar faces from school."

"People you know?" Joe asked.

"Not exactly," Chet said, shaking his head. "But the three guys that Sal seems especially chummy with—I know who they are. And guess what—they're all Starz members."

Frank narrowed his eyes. "You're sure of that?" he demanded. "That's a pretty serious allegation."

"I didn't ask to see their membership cards," Chet said. "And I didn't get close enough to see if they had those blue tattoos on their wrists. But I know them all by sight, and I know who they hang with. It was enough to make me wonder if Sal has some kind of connection to the Starz."

"Because three out of, say, twenty Freddy Frost drivers are gang members?" Joe said. "You know how it goes. Somebody gets a job. He knows when there are openings, so he tells his buddies. They apply and get jobs there, too."

"Sure, I know," Chet replied. "But I still think

it's funny that Sal's favorites all turn out to be Starz guys."

Frank tossed a piece of popcorn into his mouth. "I'm with you there, Chet," he said. "What bothers me is the fact that the guys who hijacked your truck this afternoon apparently had a key to it. They must have some close connection to Freddy Frost. And since they didn't take anything, the whole point must have been to send you a message."

"Yeah. 'Get lost—and fast,'" Chet said. "But why me? Today was my first day. I haven't had time to get under anybody's skin."

"How's this?" Joe said. "They want to scare you off. Then, when you quit, there'll be another opening that one of their friends can fill."

Chet opened a can of soda. He finished a gulp, then said, "Listen, Joe. I'm glad to have this job. I think it may even turn out to be fun. But it's not as if I'm making a fortune. I don't see people lining up around the block to take my place, never mind staging a kidnapping."

"There's another possibility, Chet," Frank said. "Everybody at Bayport High knows the three of us are friends. What if the message wasn't aimed just at you? What if Marlon Masters and his gang wanted to send a warning to all of us not to give them any trouble?"

Joe smiled grimly. "If that's the case, they sure

went about it the wrong way," he said. "Because if they start trying to lean on our friends, we're going to give them plenty of trouble!"

The next morning Joe drove the van into the school parking lot and found a space near the tennis courts. He and Frank grabbed their backpacks, locked the van, and started up the walk toward the front door.

"Uh-oh," Frank murmured. "Battle stations."

Up ahead, standing between them and the school entrance, half a dozen people were forming a solid line that blocked the whole sidewalk. At one end of the line stood Marlon Masters.

Gus French, the guy who had tangled with Joe in the lunch room the day before, moved forward to stand a pace in front of the others.

"You chumps are toast!" he said, fiddling with the studded leather band on his left wrist. "You just stuck your noses into Starz business for the last time. Now we're going to rearrange your faces. By the time we're done, you won't need a mask for Halloween.

4 Schoolyard Battleground

Even before Gus finished his threat, Frank was taking a half step to the side. He didn't want a fight, but if a fight began, he needed to give himself room. He breathed slowly and deeply, guiding his mind and body toward the state of unfocused attention of a trained martial artist. He knew that right next to him, Joe was doing the same.

Frank looked across the space that separated the Hardys from the Starz. The boy directly opposite him was about sixteen. He almost matched Frank's own six-foot-one, but his torso looked thin, as if all his strength had gone into gaining height. The boy's dark blond hair flopped over his forehead, partly hiding his small, pale blue eyes. As if he knew that Frank was watching him, he put on a fierce scowl. It didn't quite manage to conceal his nervousness, though, Frank thought.

"Let them come to us," Frank muttered to Joe out of the side of his mouth.

"Let 'em come. I'm ready anytime," Joe replied easily.

The face-off continued. With each passing second, Frank knew that he and Joe were building up more of the moral superiority that is as important in combat as physical strength. Their opponents could see that the Hardys were ready and unfrightened by the unfair odds. That knowledge was draining their own will. Unless they could bring themselves to attack in the next few moments, they would be defeated without a single blow exchanged.

Gus seemed to realize that, too. His face reddened. Clenching his fists, he took a step forward. "What are we waiting for?" he shouted. "Let's teach these suckers a lesson they won't forget!"

Frank bent his knees slightly and balanced on the balls of his feet. With so many attackers, he would need to rely on kicks to keep them at a distance.

"Wait!" a voice yelled. "Stop it!"

A woman in a green blouse and a denim skirt

came running across the schoolyard. Her shoulder-length hair was steel gray, but when Joe saw her face, he realized that she couldn't be older than thirty. Was she a teacher? He didn't think he'd ever seen her before.

The woman dashed into the space between the Hardys and the Starz that was about to become a battleground. She positioned herself directly in front of Gus. "We have a contract," she said breathlessly. "No trouble, especially not on school grounds. Remember?"

Gus looked past the woman and directly at Frank. "This is different, Hedda," he said. "We have to teach these guys respect."

"You don't teach people respect, you earn it from them," Hedda replied. She looked to her left. "Marlon, I know you understand. Tell him."

Marlon looked uncomfortable at this appeal, but after a moment he said, "Hedda's right, Gus. Beating up these guys won't prove anything. Let's go. We've got better things to do."

Marlon turned on his heel and walked toward the school entrance. The others seemed to hesitate, then they followed him. Gus was the last to go. Before leaving, he gave both Frank and Joe samples of his best dirty look.

The woman in the denim skirt watched the Starz drift away. Then she turned and walked up to Frank and Joe.

"I haven't met you fellows yet," she said. "My

33

name's Hedda Moon. I'm a counselor with an organization called Teen Peace. I'll be here at Bayport High for the next couple of months, working with young people like yourselves."

She offered her hand. Frank and Joe, in turn, shook hands and introduced themselves.

"So you're brothers," Hedda said. "I should have guessed, even if you don't look very much alike. And what's the name of your social club?"

Frank caught a confused glance from Joe. Social club? What did Hedda mean? Then it hit him. Hedda Moon must think that he and Joe were part of a teen gang like the Starz, Frank thought. He was tempted to laugh at her mistake. But that wouldn't have been polite. Instead, he said, "We're not part of a club."

"No rules, no colors, just a bunch of friends who hang together?" Hedda said, with a knowing smile. "Sure, I get it. Well, it doesn't matter. I can still help you. But you have to help me, too. You have to be willing to see your common interests with other clubs. Working together is the key. Are you with me?"

"Uh, sure," Joe said.

"And no battles like the one you almost had just now," Hedda added. "If you start beating each other up, there are no winners, only losers. And you guys don't look like losers to me."

"Thanks," Frank said. "But really, we're not—"

Hedda dug into her purse. "Here's my card," she said. "Be smart. Keep in touch with me."

As she walked away, Joe turned to Frank. "What was all that about?" he asked.

Frank explained his theory about Hedda's mistake. Joe shook his head. "Us? A gang?" he said. "That is so ridiculous!"

"Of course it is," Frank replied. "But think of it from her point of view. The two of us were standing here, and six or seven Starz were getting ready to pound on us. I can understand her mistake. What I don't understand is why Marlon and Gus wanted to sic their buddies on us."

"Maybe they think we're a gang, too," Joe suggested with a laugh. "Or—seriously—maybe they heard a rumor that the school's asked us to investigate the shakedowns."

Frank rubbed his chin. "You may have hit on something there," he said. "The sooner we find out what's going on, the better off we'll be. We've still got ten minutes before first period. Let's hunt up a few friends and ask them to keep their eyes open."

Joe headed off to look for Iola. Frank went into the building and started up to his homeroom. On the stairs, he spotted Biff Hooper talking to Tony Prito.

"Listen, you guys," he began, then told them about the near-battle with the Starz. "Do either of you know anything about them?"

"I know some of them from my classes," Biff said. "Tell you what—I'll make some notes on them and give them to you at lunch."

"Same here," Tony said. "I can tell you one thing right now. They're growing pretty fast. A couple of months ago, I only knew one guy who's a Starz. Now I know five or six."

Frank was about to reply when, over Biff's shoulder, he noticed Hedda Moon. She was watching them intently and jotting something in a small notebook. When she realized that Frank was looking at her, she put the notebook in her purse and turned to look in another direction.

Tony followed the direction of Frank's gaze. "Who's the gray-haired lady?" he asked. "A new teacher?"

Frank explained, adding, "And now I'll bet she thinks you two guys are part of the Hardy gang."

Tony just grinned.

"Fill me in later," Biff said. "The bell's going to ring any minute, and Mr. Tolbiac's been on my case about showing up late."

As the morning progressed, Frank asked friends in all his classes about the Starz. To his surprise, his question made some people very nervous. They made excuses and hurried away without answering.

Others were more willing to talk. When Frank spoke to a girl named Alesha before English class, she said, "Yeah, I know a bunch of them. And these last few weeks, I've noticed they've gotten a lot more mellow. It's like they took the chip off their shoulder."

"Why?" Frank asked her. "Any idea?"

"No question," Alesha replied, pushing her hair back behind her shoulder. "It's Marlon who's done it. That guy is one shrewd dude. If he ever gets his act together, he could end up president."

Marlon Masters, president? Frank spent the first few minutes of English class turning that idea over in his mind. He hastily put it aside when he heard Ms. Amity say, "Frank, what's your response to the point that Jenny just made? Do you think it's a fair assessment of what Hardy intended to do in this section?"

Hardy? Was the teacher talking about him? Frank wondered. About Joe? The look on Frank's face as he gradually figured out that Ms. Amity meant Thomas Hardy, the author of *Return of the Native*, made the rest of the class crack up.

After English, Frank had a free period. He decided to spend it in the library doing research for a term paper he was writing on the Civil War. His topic was the Battle of Chattanooga and the effects of the Union victory.

He had made about a half a dozen pages of notes when he realized that he needed to know more about roads and rail lines around Chattanooga, Tennessee, in 1864. Checking the card catalog, he discovered that the library had an atlas devoted to the Civil War. It was in the far corner of the room, in a special bookcase for oversize books.

Frank found the book and looked at the index to make sure that it included a map of Chattanooga. Then he headed back to the table where he had left his notebook and the history books he was consulting.

He was halfway across the room when he saw that someone was standing at his place, bending over his books, with his back to Frank. Could it be a classmate trying to copy his notes? Frank wondered. He walked faster.

The person seemed to sense Frank's approach. Without looking around, he straightened up and hurried out of the library.

Now Frank was really beginning to worry. He lengthened his stride to cover the last twenty feet to the table.

"Oh, no!" he groaned.

His notebook and the two valuable reference books he had been consulting had been smeared with a thick coating of white paste.

5 Sidelined

For a moment Frank was too shocked by the sight of the vandalism to react. Then he grabbed his book bag, found a packet of tissues, and began to mop at the still-damp paste. Some of it came up, but in places the tissue tore off and stuck to the page.

A shadow moved across the book he was scrubbing. Frank glanced up. A bearded man was glaring at him. The photo ID pinned to his shirt pocket read Walter Winger. Frank thought he recalled seeing him behind the library checkout desk earlier.

"What is this mess?" Winger hissed. "Do you realize what you've done? Here, give me that!"

He reached for the book Frank was working on and pulled it away.

"I didn't do anything," Frank protested. "Somebody put paste on the pages. On my notes, too. See?"

"I'll take care of these," Winger continued, paying no attention to what Frank had said. He picked up the second damaged book. "As for you, I'm sending you to the principal's office. And I'll call ahead to be sure that Ms. Carl is expecting you and knows why you're there. Where's your student card?"

Frank produced his ID. Winger checked the photo against Frank's face, then noted his name and student number on an index card. "All right, Frank Hardy," he said in a grim tone. "Get moving. And don't be surprised if your library privileges are suspended for the rest of the quarter. These books are meant to be used by students who know how to care for them."

Frank slung his backpack over his left shoulder and picked up his notebook, holding it open to the vandalized pages. If Winger didn't want to know about it, Frank still hoped that he might manage to find someone in Ms. Carl's office who would listen.

As Frank entered the outer office, the secretary gave him a hard look. "I've just had Mr. Winger on the line," she said. "You'll have to see Ms.

Carl. Destruction of school property is a very serious offense."

She picked up the phone, punched the intercom button, and spoke in a voice too low for Frank to hear. Then she said, "Ms. Carl will see you now."

The principal was standing at the windows, which looked out over the roof of the cafeteria and the tennis courts. When Frank entered, she turned to face him. She was a woman in her forties, with shoulder-length blond hair and blue eyes that usually had a touch of amusement in them.

"Well, Frank Hardy," she said lightly. "What is one-half of Bayport High's famous team of detectives doing pouring glue on library books? Is that some new method for picking up fingerprints?"

Frank felt some of the tension in his shoulders drain away. At least Ms. Carl hadn't already decided that he had vandalized the books himself. He explained what had happened and showed her his notebook.

"Why would someone do that?" Ms. Carl asked. "I'm not questioning your story, Frank. But I wonder what the motive could be."

"Somebody doesn't like me," Frank replied. "Or doesn't like something I've done or might do."

"Did you get a good look at the person who did it?" Ms. Carl continued.

"I was halfway across the room, and his back was to me," Frank replied.

"Hmm . . ." Ms. Carl put one knuckle against her lower lip for a few moments. Then she asked, "Mr. Vincenza spoke to you yesterday, didn't he?"

Surprised, Frank said, "That's right."

"Do you think what happened to you just now has any connection with the investigation he asked you and your brother to take on?"

"I don't really know," Frank admitted. "It's possible, of course. But sometimes things just happen. I don't have a solid reason to think it's a gang member or anyone in particular, for that matter."

"I see," Ms. Carl said. She crossed to her desk and picked up the phone. After a couple of sentences too low for Frank to overhear, she looked over at him and said, "Frank, would you mind stopping by Mr. Vincenza's office for a moment when you leave here?"

"Sure," Frank said. "But what—"

"He'll explain," Ms. Carl replied. "Oh, and don't worry—I'll let Walter Winger know that you're not the danger he thought you were."

Frank left the office. What he hadn't told Ms. Carl—what he couldn't tell her—was that he had gotten a quick glimpse of the person who had smeared paste on the books. All he had seen was his back, but even so, he was pretty sure that the culprit was Gus French.

The door to Mr. Vincenza's office was ajar. Frank tapped on it.

"Come on in," Mr. Vincenza called from behind his desk. "Hi, Frank. Close the door, would you? Take a seat," he said, gesturing to the chair beside his desk.

Once Frank was seated, Mr. Vincenza said, "I was planning to hunt up you and Joe at lunchtime, but Ms. Carl saved me the trouble."

"Is anything wrong?" Frank asked.

"Just the opposite," Mr. Vincenza replied. "First of all, I want you to know how much I appreciate how ready you fellows were to help out with the problem we've been having. And I'm happy to be able to say that we won't need to impose on you after all."

"Why is that?" Frank asked, puzzled.

"By a wonderful coincidence, we're going to have a professional to deal with it," Mr. Vincenza said. He leaned back in his chair and folded his hands. "Have you heard of an organization called Teen Peace? They've offered to lend us the services of a highly trained counselor, a woman named Hedda Moon. I've already asked her to see what she can do about the problem I told you about yesterday. So you and Joe can relax."

"But, Mr. Vincenza, we were starting to get

somewhere in our investigation," Frank protested.

"I'm glad to hear it," Mr. Vincenza said with a smile. "Still, it's great that now we have someone with training to take care of it. We don't want to take your minds off your schoolwork, do we?"

Too late, Frank thought grimly, as his mind went back to the near-attack from the Starz members before school that morning.

English was Joe's last class before lunch. The topic was a poem by Robert Frost. Joe tried to concentrate on what Mr. Bennett, the teacher, and his classmates were saying, but he couldn't. He was too aware of Marlon Masters, two rows away, and the dirty looks he kept shooting Joe's way.

It was strange, Joe thought. Until today, he had never had any problems with Marlon. Now it seemed as if they had turned into enemies. What had happened.

The bell rang. As Joe put his notebook away and stood up, Marlon came over to his desk. Joe faced him and waited.

"There's talk around school," Marlon said. "The word is that you and your brother are spreading lies about the Starz. You're trying to pin something on us. I don't know what, and I don't know why. But I'm here to tell you, it won't work."

"And I've got something to tell you," Joe said.

44

"Frank and I aren't doing anything. It seems as if you're really the ones looking for trouble. Who was it who tried to start something this morning? Not us, Marlon, and you know it."

Marlon's eyes narrowed. "I've heard about you and your friends. You think you're so hot. Frank and Joe Hardy, boy detectives," he added in a singsong voice. "Oh, I'm so scared. You tangle with the Starz, and you're going to find out what it's like to be scared."

Joe couldn't help it. He started laughing. Marlon's face reddened. He grabbed Joe's shirtfront with his left hand and pulled back the right hand, ready to throw a punch. Joe thrust his crossed forearms upward, breaking the hold and blocking the blow. Taken by surprise, Marlon recoiled. Joe twisted at the waist, ready to follow through with a disabling elbow strike to his attacker.

"Hold it!" Mr. Bennett forced himself between Joe and Marlon. "Are you both out of your minds? You're looking at a week's suspension if you keep this up."

Joe was about to say, "He started it." Then he realized how childish that would sound. Instead, he lowered his hands and took a step backward. After a tiny pause, Marlon did the same.

"That's better," Mr. Bennett said. "And don't think you can start up again as soon as you're out of my classroom. Marlon, you leave first."

Joe opened his mouth to protest. Then he caught a glance from Mr. Bennett. "Okay," he said.

Marlon walked away without another word or glance in Joe's direction. But Joe could tell that the argument was far from over.

"Now, Joe, what's going on?" Mr. Bennett demanded. "I had the impression that Marlon was trying to pick a fight with you."

"I guess," Joe said, looking at the floor.

"And that you were all too ready to give him what he wanted," Mr. Bennett continued.

"I'm sorry," Joe muttered. "I lost my cool."

"Please try to find it again," Mr. Bennett said. "You have more influence on your fellow students than you may realize. I'd like to see you use it wisely. Marlon has a lot of effect, too. He's a very strong character. But I'm afraid he may be headed in the wrong direction. Do you know anything about that?"

Joe hesitated. He liked and respected Mr. Bennett. But telling tales to a teacher about a fellow student went against his principles—certainly not without solid evidence of wrongdoing.

"Not really," Joe said. "I guess he has a bone to pick with me, that's all."

Mr. Bennett gave Joe a piercing look, then said, "Okay, Joe, off with you. I won't keep you from lunch. But I hope you'll feel free to come to me at any time, especially if there's something you'd like to talk about."

"Oh, sure, Mr. Bennett," Joe said. "You bet."

As he went downstairs to the cafeteria, Joe stayed alert. He didn't seriously expect Marlon to jump him in the hallway, but Joe decided to be ready for anything.

Once in line at the cafeteria, he put Marlon out of his thoughts temporarily to ponder the day's choice for the main dish: spaghetti with tomato sauce or breaded veal patties. He chose the spaghetti and headed for the usual table.

Frank and the others were already sitting down when Joe arrived. "We've been yanked off the case," Frank said in a low voice as Joe took a seat next to his brother.

"What?" Joe said, startled. "Why?"

"The school brought in an expert," Frank told him. "And guess who it is? Hedda Moon, that woman who stepped in this morning when the Starz wanted to flatten us."

"That stinks!" Joe said. "Just when we're getting somewhere, they call in some grown-up with a degree."

Frank glanced around, then said, "I say we stay on the case. But we'll have to be careful. We can't let Mr. Vincenza know what we're doing."

"Fine with me," Joe said as he twirled a long strand of spaghetti on his fork.

"Tony," Frank said, joining the conversation

47

with the rest of the table, "what about the Starz members you checked out?"

Tony rattled off a list of names, then added, "I didn't think I'd know so many, Frank. And there's a lot more people who aren't members but who go along with the Starz—probably because they're afraid not to."

"I found out the same thing," Iola said. "People I asked didn't want to talk about the Starz. Even the ones who did kept looking over their shoulders."

Chet put down his fork and leaned forward. "We have to be careful, though. I know the Starz act like a gang. But that doesn't prove they're criminals. Nobody I talked to could link them to any particular thing that's been going on at school."

Joe swallowed a mouthful of spaghetti. "What about all the shakedowns?" he said. "And the stuff taken from people's lockers? You think that was *not* done by the Starz?"

"I know about that, Joe," Chet said. "But that was weeks ago, before anybody even heard of the Starz. Since then, things have gotten better. And anyway, what I'm saying is that there's nothing solid to connect the Starz with those crimes."

Joe threw up his hands. "Okay, maybe they're really a charity organization," he said. "But I say we find out for sure."

"Maybe I can help," Callie said. "There's this

girl, Stephanie, in my Spanish class. She just broke up with her boyfriend, who's a big deal in the Starz. She's pretty mad about it, too. I can't promise anything—I don't know her that well—but I think I can get her to talk to me. I'm sure she knows a lot about what's going on."

"Go, Callie," Frank said. "But be careful. If we're right about the Starz, and they start to catch on to what you're doing, it could be dangerous."

Joe was about to start eating his dessert when he realized that he'd forgotten to get a spoon. Mumbling "I'll be right back," he pushed his chair away from the table.

With no warning, the corner of a tray slammed into his back. The next thing anyone knew, a steaming plate of spaghetti and tomato sauce slid off the tray and flipped over onto Callie's lap.

6 Hedda Steps In

Callie screamed when the spaghetti cascaded onto her lap. She jumped out of her chair and frantically brushed at her jeans. At the surrounding tables, people turned and stared, trying to see what the commotion was about. Frank grabbed his napkin and helped Callie mop off some of the mess. Iola dashed to the service counter and returned with a handful of paper towels. Moments later one of the cafeteria staff arrived with a mop and started to clean up the floor.

Frank saw that Callie was trembling. "Here, sit down," he said, and took her elbow.

"I'm all right," Callie said, but her voice shook. "It just took me by surprise, that's all."

"Why don't you let me drive you home, so you can change?" Frank offered. "We'd be back before lunch period is over."

Callie shook her head. "No, I'm all right, really. There's a pair of sweatpants in my locker. I can put them on."

"Oh, good," Iola said. "I guess it just shows that accidents happen. But I'm surprised that guy ran off like that. Why didn't he stick around to help clean up the mess he made? You'd think he could at least apologize."

"*I'm* not surprised," Callie told her. "Remember, I was telling you about Stephanie, who just broke up with a Starz member? Well, that's the guy—Dino—who just dumped his lunch on me. Accident? I don't think so."

Frank felt anger course through him. He scanned the lunch room. Dino was standing over near the doors. He was laughing and trading high fives with a cluster of guys. One of them was Gus French.

"I'll be right back," Frank growled. "After I've taken care of some urgent business."

Fists clenched, Frank stalked across the room. He was a dozen feet from the group of Starz when Hedda Moon blocked his way.

"Wait, Frank," she said, holding up her hand like a traffic cop. "I need to talk to you."

"I'm sorry, it'll have to wait," Frank said, more gruffly than he intended to. "I'm busy."

51

He tried to step around her, but she sidestepped, too. "No, Frank. Now," she said in a firm voice. "Before you make things worse."

"Worse than dumping a hot lunch on my girlfriend?" Frank demanded.

"Much worse," Hedda replied. "I saw the whole thing. Your brother got up from the table and bumped into Dino's tray. Dino couldn't help it. He wasn't trying to start something. But you, Frank—you *are* planning to start something. I want to keep that from happening."

Frank looked past Hedda. Dino, Gus, and the other Starz members were walking out of the cafeteria, still laughing among themselves. Thanks to Hedda's interference, Frank thought in disgust, the moment had passed.

Besides, what if Hedda was right? Frank thought. What if the spill really had been an accident? He didn't believe it for a moment, but then again he didn't want to start a fistfight over an accident. And anyway, he concluded with a sigh, he'd already paid one visit to the principal's office. That was his quota for the day.

"I'm deeply concerned about the rising tension here at Bayport High," Hedda was saying. "Something has to be done about it, and quickly. I have a meeting this afternoon with Marlon and his friends. I'm going to see to it they agree to a cooling-off period."

Frank gave Hedda a cool, disbelieving stare.

Hedda's cheeks turned pink. "I mean it, Frank," she said. "In the long run, I've found them to be reasonable. I hope I will this time, too. But compromise is a two-way street. I need help from you and your organization, as well."

"I don't *have* an organization!" Frank said, his voice rising in frustration.

"You and your friends, then," Hedda said quickly. "You have to do your part. The whole school knows about your spying and prying. You've got to stop it. What the Starz do is their business, not yours. When they see your . . . friends going around talking to anyone who might have a grudge against them, it makes them nervous. It makes them wonder if you're going to try to pin something on them. Some false charge that will damage their reputation. You wouldn't like it if somebody was doing that to you, would you?"

"Look, we're not trying to pin anything on the Starz," Frank said. "They're the ones who've been trying to pick a fight with us!"

"That's the terrible thing about conflicts." Hedda sighed. "So often, both sides are sure that the other is out to get them. That's why it's so important for each of you see the other point of view—to see the benefits of real cooperation. When I speak to Marlon, I'm going to suggest

53

that the Starz have a sit-down with you and your friends to work out your difficulties. Tomorrow, if possible. What do you say? Is it a deal?"

Frank hesitated. He didn't think that he and Joe had much to say to Marlon and his gang. On the other hand, if he turned down an offer of a peace conference, he would make it look as if he were in the wrong. "Well . . . okay," he said finally.

Hedda reached out to shake Frank's hand. "That's the right choice, Frank," she said. "You'll see. For now, stay cool and increase the peace."

When Frank returned to the table, Callie and Iola had left. Joe gave him a curious look. "What were you doing over there?" he asked.

"I was letting myself be talked into a meeting with the Starz," Frank replied. "Hedda Moon is a very persuasive lady. She thinks we should negotiate a truce with them."

"The nerve," Tony said, his face flushed. "I'd like to negotiate some knuckles on that guy Dino's nose."

"Now, now, Tony, that's not a productive attitude," Chet said, pretending to sound like Hedda. "Aren't you mature enough to realize that senseless violence is, uh, senseless?"

In response, Tony aimed a playful punch at Chet's midsection. Chet dodged it.

"Seriously, guys," Joe said. "We don't want to

start a war with the Starz. We don't need to respond in any way to this incident. But if they're involved in any criminal activity, that's something else. It's our right and our duty to track it down and expose it."

"So we go on with the investigation," Biff said. "Good. I'm getting tired of the way those hoods have people around here buffaloed. Oops," he said looking at the large clock on the wall of the cafeteria. "I'd better run. I'll be late for language lab. I hate it when I'm stuck with a tape machine that makes everything sound like my dad gargling with mouthwash."

Frank and the others stood up, too. Frank said, "We never finished pooling what we've found out so far. Let's meet out front near the flagpole after school, okay? We can figure out where to go next."

"Good idea," Joe said. Biff and Tony agreed.

"Sorry, guys, I can't," Chet said. "I have to go straight to Freddy Frost to pick up my truck. But I'll talk to you tonight. Say," he added as he picked up his tray, "what do you think of lasagna sherbet?"

"As little as possible," Frank said. "If anyone runs into Callie and Iola, tell them about the meeting."

On the way out of the cafeteria, Frank told Joe about the incident in the library and more details of his conversation with Mr. Vincenza.

"How could it not have been one of the Starz who did it?" Joe said hotly.

"I agree," Frank replied. "You know, if we proceed with our investigation, we're on our own. We won't have any help from any school officials. Is it worth taking that big a chance?"

"You're asking me—after all that has happened to us today?" Joe replied. "I want to see those creeps get what they deserve . . . and I don't mean a nice talk with some wimpy counselor!"

When school ended, Joe was the first to reach the flagpole. He couldn't wait to talk to the others. A couple of minutes later Callie showed up.

"Oh!" she said. "I am so furious I could spit nails!"

"Let me guess," Joe replied. "Somebody crashed into you in the hall."

"Three times," Callie said, tight-lipped. "Always from behind. And in Spanish, when I got up to sharpen my pencil, I came back and found my looseleaf binder on the floor—with the rings open. It took me ten minutes to get the pages back in order. I'm starting to know what a punching bag must feel like."

"Yeah, same here," Joe said. "I had to work hard not to lose my temper, especially after somebody spilled acid on my chemistry notes. And then, when some guy tried to trip me in the hall a little while ago, I lost my balance."

"You, Joe Hardy?" Callie exclaimed. "Come on—I've seen you on the football field. You never lose your balance."

Joe grinned at the compliment. "It's true, though. And when I started to fall, my heel ended up right on the toes of the guy who tripped me. I tried to apologize. But I'm afraid he was yelling too loudly to hear what I was saying."

Iola, Biff, and Frank joined them. Moments later Tony hurried up. "I can't stay," he said breathlessly. "I just checked in at the pizzeria. Somebody called them a little while ago and said I'd be taking today and tomorrow off. My boss nearly went ballistic. He was counting on me."

"Why are they doing this to us?" Iola cried, as Tony rushed off. "What have we done to them?"

Biff shrugged. "Nothing. Maybe they just don't like us," he suggested. "It stands to reason. I don't like *them*."

"Or maybe having somebody to be against keeps them together," Iola said.

"You may both be right," Frank said. "But let's not forget how this all started. Twenty-four hours ago we'd barely heard of the Starz. And I doubt if they'd heard of us."

57

"So what started it?" Biff asked.

"Chet's new job at Freddy Frost," Joe said. "That's what you were getting at, isn't it, Frank?"

"It looks that way to me," Frank said. "We know that some Starz members are driving Freddy Frost trucks. When Chet started work there, maybe they figured he was moving in on what they see as their territory. That abduction on Chet's first day of his job was supposed to be a warning. Today they decided that it wasn't just Chet—that all of us were part of it. So they started a campaign to scare us off."

"Why?" Biff asked. "Driving a Freddy Frost truck sounds like a good job, but I doubt if you make a fortune at it. So why make a big deal out of keeping other people out?"

"I have an idea on that," Callie said. "Frank, I don't think you and Joe realize how much clout you two have around here. Everybody at Bayport High knows about you and your crime-fighting. So when one of your close friends started working for Freddy Frost, it must have felt like a direct challenge. For a guy like Marlon, that kind of challenge puts his own prestige on the line. He's got to respond to it."

"That's right," Iola said excitedly. "And if he can make kids think that Joe and Frank Hardy are afraid to stand up to him, who else is going to dream of trying?"

Joe felt his cheeks grow warm. It embarrassed

him to hear friends like Iola and Callie make a big deal of the success he and Frank had had as detectives. It was just something they did, that was all.

To avoid the look of admiration in Iola's eyes, Joe turned his head and gazed across the lawn toward the hedge surrounding the school parking lot.

A blue station wagon shot out from behind the hedge, its tires smoking. It was filled with boys. The car stopped for a split second, and one of the boys jumped out and hurled something in the direction of the Hardys and their friends. A bottle came hurtling in their direction. Before they could run for cover, the bottle shattered on the sidewalk at their feet, and shards of glass flew in all directions.

7 The Inside Scoop

"Dive behind the bushes, everyone!" Joe shouted.

Iola was standing closest to Joe. He grabbed her by the arm and pulled her to the side. An instant later a second bottle shattered on the sidewalk where the group had been standing. Two other bottles followed closely. Splinters of glass sprayed the area. Biff let out a shout of pain.

Frank was already sprinting toward the parking lot. Joe paused just long enough to make sure that Biff wasn't badly hurt. Then he dashed after Frank. The blue station wagon was already racing toward the street, tires squealing. One of its passengers was looking out the back window with a smirk. Joe recognized Gus French and made a promise to himself to wipe the grin off the guy's face at the first opportunity.

"Come on," Joe said to Frank. "Let's make sure that everyone's okay."

"Wait a sec," Frank replied. "I think I see the red car that was following us. Let's do something before he can get away."

Joe and Frank ran toward the red car. The same man in sunglasses was at the wheel. Frank could see the man's mouth drop open in surprise when he saw the Hardys. A moment later the car's engine started up. But before it could move, Joe leaped onto the hood and lay spread-eagled on the windshield. Meanwhile, Frank was jerking the driver's door open.

"Hey, what is this?" the driver demanded loudly. "What do you boys want?"

"A little chat, that's all," Frank told him. "Why don't you turn off your engine and get out of the car?"

Joe climbed down from the hood and joined Frank by the open car door.

"No way," the man replied. "And if you try to pull me out, I'll have you arrested for assault."

"Do you have a school parking permit?" Joe retorted. "If not, *we* can have *you* arrested for trespassing."

The man gave a short laugh. "Sounds like a standoff," he said. He reached forward and switched off the ignition. "So, now what?"

"You can start by telling us who you are," Frank said.

"And why you've been tailing us," Joe added.

Joe tensed as the man reached inside his jacket. Was he about to draw a gun? But when his hand reappeared, all it was holding was a business card. He passed it to Frank, who held it out for Joe to see, too.

"'Aaron McCay, Investigative Reporter,'" Joe read aloud. "Sounds like a good name for a TV show."

"Thanks," McCay said proudly. "You never know . . . maybe one of these days."

"What paper do you work for, Mr. McCay?" Frank asked.

"I'm freelance," McCay told them. "I write for a lot of different publications."

"And which of them wants you to investigate us?" Joe asked.

"You boys have it all wrong," McCay proclaimed. "Look, here's the way it is. I've been working on a feature story about the after-school activities of local high school students. You know—sports, interesting hobbies, part-time jobs—things like that. Then I heard about a couple of guys who are amateur detectives. I told myself, 'They're a natural.' You catch my drift?"

"I think so," Frank said sarcastically. He tucked McCay's card into his shirt pocket.

"I want to see to it that you boys get the fame you deserve," McCay continued. "Here's my idea. You let me follow you around and take notes on your next investigation. When it's finished, I'll write it in the form of an adventure story. Don't worry, I'll change the names and some of the details, to keep from embarrassing anybody. I'll bet it'll be a big hit. In fact, it wouldn't surprise me if the publishers decided to do a whole series of books about you. What do you say?"

"My brother and I would have to think that one over," Frank said. "But I can't help wondering—if you were planning to approach us with this idea, why did you try so hard to avoid us yesterday and again this afternoon?"

McCay looked flustered. He bit his lower lip, then said, "Oh, um . . . I wanted to get a start on my project before I told you about it. That way, you'd realize that I was making a serious proposition." He added quickly, "Which I am."

"So you admit following us yesterday," Joe said.

"I just told you so," McCay replied. "Look, this isn't getting us anywhere. Do we have a deal?"

Joe ignored his question and asked, "Those guys who were throwing bottles at us just now— could you identify them if you saw them again?"

"Throwing bottles?" McCay looked down at

his dashboard. "Sorry, fellows. I don't know what you're talking about. I was just sitting here going through my notes. I didn't see anything."

Joe put his head inside the car and scanned the front seat. There was no sign of any notes. The back of McCay's neck turned red.

"You don't have to believe me," McCay said belligerently.

"That's a good thing," Joe replied. "If you weren't watching those bottle throwers, what were you doing here?"

"Working on a story," McCay insisted. "And that's all I'm going to say. Look, I'm offering to make you guys a household name. It's a legitimate offer. But as they say on television, it's a limited-time offer. If you don't want to cooperate with me, too bad for you. Maybe I'll find somebody else who's more reasonable. There's two sides to every story, you know. And I can tell it either way."

Joe looked over at Frank, who gave a thin smile and said, "We'll keep that in mind, Mr. McCay. And if you happen to remember anything that might be helpful—about those bottle throwers, for instance—please let us know."

Joe and Frank stepped back. McCay slammed his door closed, started his engine, and drove off.

"Come on," Frank said. "We'd better make sure everybody's okay."

The Hardys returned to the flagpole and their friends. Biff had a scratch on his cheek from a piece of flying glass, but neither Callie nor Iola was hurt.

"What happened to you guys?" Callie asked. "You were gone so long, we were starting to worry."

Frank told them about their encounter with Aaron McCay.

"Weird," Biff commented. "How good a reporter could he be if he didn't catch the bottle-throwing scene? He was practically in the middle of it."

"I wonder what he meant about every story having two sides and that he could tell it either way," Iola said.

"I have a hunch about that," Joe told her. "I think he must be in touch with Marlon or some of the other Starz. If we don't let him make us the heroes of his story, he's planning to make *them* the heroes and us the bad guys."

"But that wouldn't be honest!" Callie exclaimed.

Frank laughed. "I guess we shouldn't believe everything we read in the papers, then. But, you know," he added, "McCay may have stumbled on some useful information. I wonder how we can find out."

"What if we pretend to go along with his

scheme about a series of books?" Joe suggested. "We give him a few tiny facts about the case, then tell him it's his turn."

"Good idea," Frank said. "Maybe he'll help us figure out what this case is about. The Starz are trying very hard to scare us away, but away from what?"

"I'll call Stephanie when I get home to see if we can get together. I'll see what I can find out," Callie offered.

"I'll do whatever needs doing," Biff said. "But right now I have to split. I promised Mom I'd run some errands for her this afternoon."

After Biff left, the Hardys dropped off Callie and Iola, then headed home themselves. As they entered the kitchen, their mother, Laura Hardy, greeted them. "Someone called for you a few minutes ago," she said. "A man. He wouldn't leave his name, but he said something about seeing you in Jefferson Park. I hope that makes sense to you."

Joe met Frank's eyes, then said, "Sort of."

"Another case?" Mrs. Hardy asked. "I don't have to tell you to be careful. You may be nearly grown, but you're still my little boys."

Red-faced, Joe mumbled, "Sure, Mom. We'll be careful."

He and Frank made sandwiches, filled a bowl with chips, grabbed some sodas, then went to boot up the computer. A few minutes of on-line searching confirmed that Aaron McCay really was a writer. Apparently he had done everything from science fiction novels to a collection of traditional recipes from Nebraska. His most recent articles had appeared in a weekly paper that specialized in sensational stories about events in the Bayport area.

"Do you think he was the one who called and talked to Mom?" Joe asked.

"He was watching us yesterday at Jefferson Park," Frank pointed out. "Who else saw us there?"

"Wait a minute," Joe said. "Maybe whoever left the message didn't mean that he *had* seen us there. What if he meant that he *wants* to see us there?"

Frank shrugged. "Then why didn't he say so? And even if he did, I don't feel like running all over town just because that guy says jump."

"I think we should go take a look," Joe said.

Frank shook his head. "You go if you want. I'm going to take the information everybody gathered about the Starz and try to put it into some kind of order."

Frank picked up his sheaf of notes and turned back to the computer. Joe hesitated for a moment, then said, "Okay. I'll see you later."

As Joe left the house, he noticed his mountain bike leaning against the wall in the garage. He loved to ride it, but what with the van, he never got around to it. Why not now, he decided? It wouldn't take him much longer to get to Jefferson Park than if he drove the van. He strapped on his helmet, hopped onto the bike, and took off.

Joe was enjoying the ride across town so much that as he neared the park, he had to remind himself that this was business. He scanned the parked cars for a red compact and checked out the few pedestrians for any sign of McCay or anyone who looked familiar.

Joe circled the park twice, then cut across it on each of the diagonal walks. The park was peaceful and quiet, except near the playground, where half a dozen kids were playing tag. Joe paused to watch a little girl throwing a Frisbee to her cocker spaniel. The dog was adept at catching the Frisbee in midair.

It was getting on toward dinnertime. Joe finally admitted that, from the point of view of the case, his ride to the park had turned out to be a bust. Still, he'd gotten some fresh air and a good workout, so it hadn't been a total waste, he concluded.

He rode across the sidewalk onto the street and turned toward home. He had gone a little over half a block when, from behind him, he heard a familiar tinkling melody. A Freddy Frost truck was coming. Grinning, Joe glanced over his shoulder, hoping to see Chet.

The ice-cream truck was a couple of dozen yards behind him. The sun visor hid the driver's face. Joe realized that the truck was picking up speed and heading straight at him. The grin froze on his face. He began pedaling hard as the truck bore down on him.

8 Danger on Wheels

The Freddy Frost truck was only yards behind Joe now. Joe swerved sharply to the right, pulled up on the handlebars, and jumped the curb. The mountain bike wobbled as the front tire skidded on the grass. Joe gave the pedals a hard push to straighten up. He raced onto the sidewalk, then risked another hasty glance over his shoulder.

The Freddy Frost truck lurched over the curb onto the sidewalk behind Joe. The glare of the sun on the windshield kept Joe from seeing the driver's face, but he had no doubt about the driver's purpose. As he put all his strength into a desperate sprint, Joe looked around quickly for refuge.

The front yard of the house just ahead of him sloped gently up to the front door. The lawn was smooth and wide. He would have no trouble riding up the lawn, but the Freddy Frost truck could follow just as easily, he realized.

Joe let out a grunt of relief when he saw the next house down. A thick chest-high hedge bordered the driveway. On the far side of the hedge was the massive trunk of an oak tree. Let the truck driver try to get past that, Joe thought triumphantly!

He knew surprise was essential. Pedaling rapidly, Joe waited until he was even with the driveway. Then he jerked the handlebars around and threw his weight to the right. Unbalanced, the bike went into a full power slide, turning ninety degrees in less than two feet of forward motion.

As the tip of the right pedal dug into the grass, Joe flung himself off the bike, did a forward tuck-and-roll, and ended up crouched in the shelter of the tree trunk. Only moments later the Freddy Frost truck sideswiped the hedge, slowed for an instant, then careered back into the street and roared away.

From the nearest house, a man in khaki work clothes came rushing out. "Hey, what's going on?" he shouted, staring at the deep ruts from the truck tires. "Look what that idiot did to my lawn!"

Joe used the tree trunk to help pull himself to his feet. His left knee hurt, his T-shirt had a new rip in it, and he had banged his wrist on the handlebars. Not good, but a lot better than going under a speeding truck, he thought grimly.

"Are you all right?" the man in khaki said as he noticed Joe.

"I'll be okay," Joe told him, though he knew he'd be limping slightly for a few days.

"I'm going to report that truck to the police," the man declared. "Talk about reckless driving—he could have hit you!"

"Yeah, I know," Joe said. He picked up his bike and checked it for damage, adding to himself under his breath, "He sure tried his best to."

"Are you sure you're all right?" the man repeated as Joe mounted his bicycle and prepared to ride off.

"I'll be fine, thanks," Joe said, and pushed off. He wanted to get home as quickly as possible. Wait until Frank hears about this! Joe thought.

Frank listened intently to Joe's account of his narrow escape. When Joe finished, he asked, "Did you get a look at the driver?"

Joe shook his head. "Afraid not. But I got something almost as good. I saw the truck's registration number. It was one-seven-four."

"Good going!" Frank said. He checked the

directory, then reached for the telephone. He cleared his throat as the phone rang, then in his best adult voice he said, "Hello, is this the Freddy Frost Company? A little while ago I bought an ice cream from one of your trucks, and I'd like to write a note to the driver telling him what a good job he's doing. Can you tell me his name, please? It was number one-seven-four . . . Oh, really? You're sure? Okay, thanks."

Frank hung up the phone and turned back to Joe. "Truck one-seven-four is assigned to Chet Morton," he reported.

Joe's jaw dropped. "Chet?" he repeated. "That's impossible? He'd never pull a dangerous stunt like that. Maybe I read the number wrong."

"Or maybe it was Chet's truck, but somebody else was at the wheel," Frank said. "It's too bad you didn't see the driver. I wouldn't mind knowing if he happened to be wearing a ski mask."

Joe jumped up and reached for his jacket. "Let's go over to the plant to see if we can find the truck," he said. "Maybe there'll be some clue to the person who was driving it."

The Freddy Frost factory was an old two-story building in an industrial park on the west side of Bayport. Its neighbors included a gasoline bulk plant, a furniture warehouse, and a plumbing company. A high chain-link fence encircled the asphalt parking lot, where a couple of dozen ice-cream trucks stood in neat rows.

The guard booth at the main gate was empty. "Tight security," Joe remarked as he drove through and parked near the waiting trucks.

The Hardys climbed out of the van and walked down between the rows of trucks. The fourth on the left was number 174. It looked newer and shinier than most of the others.

"Which side of the truck hit the hedge?" Frank asked.

"The right," Joe replied. "That's funny—I don't see any scratches. Do you?"

"Nope," Frank said. "But look at the one next to it—number two-one-three. There's a bunch of horizontal scratches on the right front fender. They look fresh, too."

Joe joined Frank in examining the other truck. He knelt down on the pavement and peered at the underside of the front bumper. "Look at this," he said, straightening up. In his hand was a tiny sprig of green leaves. "This was caught in the bumper mount."

Frank examined the leaves. Then he walked to the rear of the truck and stared at the number painted there from several angles. Finally he said, "If you catch the light just right, you can see two thin lines of adhesive, just above and below the number."

74

"You see what that means, don't you?" Joe replied. "Somebody must have taped a fake number over the real one. Now all we need to do is find out who was driving this truck."

Frank made a wry face. "I don't think I can pull the phone-call trick again," he said. "How many calls do you think they get from satisfied customers on a normal day?"

"They must keep a duty roster or something," Joe pointed out. "All we need is a look at it."

The Hardys walked across the parking lot to the plant entrance. They went inside through a pair of big sliding doors and entered a glassed-in office. A man with thinning black hair was standing by the desk, looking down at a clipboard. He heard the Hardys' footsteps and looked up. His droopy cheeks, downturned mouth, and bags under his eyes reminded Frank of a basset hound. All he lacked were the long ears.

"If you're looking for work, we're full up for now," the man said. "You can leave your applications if you want. We'll call you if something opens up."

Frank took a chance and said, "Are you Mr. Vitello?"

"That's me," the man responded. "And you are . . . ?"

"Frank Hardy, and this is my brother, Joe," Frank said. He offered Vitello his hand. As they

75

shook, he moved a little to the left. Vitello moved with him. That left him with his back mostly to the desk. "Did Chet Morton mention us to you?"

Vitello looked puzzled. "Morton? Oh, yeah—the kid who started yesterday. Nope, he didn't say a word. What's up?"

Frank started a long rambling explanation about a project for the Economics Club at Bayport High. He and his brother were going to make an in-depth report on a successful local business, and they wanted to do Freddy Frost.

As he spoke, he continued to inch to his left. Vitello moved to continue facing him. Meanwhile, Joe wandered aimlessly around the office, looking at the posters on the walls, the bowling team trophies on the bookcase, and the truck assignment sheet that was sitting on the desk. Finally he gave Frank a thumbs-up sign.

"Anyway, that's what we'd like to do," Frank concluded. "You don't have to decide now. We're just getting under way."

"You'd better give me something in writing," Vitello said. "It's not my decision, anyway. I'd have to check it with my boss."

"Oh, we understand that," Frank assured him. He noticed a file on the desk marked Flavor Contest. He pointed to it. "Hey, Chet told us about the contest. Is it too late to enter?"

76

"Tomorrow's the last day," Vitello said. "The boss is going to look over the entries tomorrow night and pick the winner. But he's already talking about running another contest, maybe even next month."

"Neat," Frank said. "Well, thanks for your time. We'll be in touch."

He and Joe left the building and walked quickly to their van.

"Well?" Frank asked, as they pulled out of the parking lot.

Joe looked over and gave him a satisfied smile. "Truck two-one-three was signed out by Gus French," he said. "That call Mom got about Jefferson Park must have been part of a trap set by the Starz."

Frank thought about that. It was the phone call that had drawn Joe to Jefferson Park. Once there, he was nearly run over by a Freddy Frost truck that had been deliberately disguised to implicate Chet. So far, so good, he thought, but something didn't quite fit.

"Joe?" Frank said. "Gus couldn't have known *when* one of us would show up at the park. And he certainly couldn't have known that you'd show up on your bike. And let's face it—a Freddy Frost truck is pretty conspicuous. You can't just park it somewhere and wait. People would notice and wonder about it."

"Okay," Joe said. "But where does that take us?"

"You said the attack came quite a while after you got to the park," Frank explained. "In fact, when you were on your way back home. Why not earlier? Because Gus had to find out that you had gone there, then get there himself. In other words, he had an accomplice who watched our house, tailed you to the park, and then let him know you were there. You didn't happen to notice any red cars hanging around, did you, when you left our house?"

Joe bit his lower lip angrily. "I checked when I got to the park, but I didn't check at our house or along the way to the park," he confessed. "When I'm driving, I usually keep an eye on who's behind me. It's second nature. But on a bike? I could have had a whole circus parade on my tail and not noticed it. You think McCay is in league with the Starz, then?"

"I don't know," Frank said. "But I wouldn't be surprised. He's up to something, that's clear."

They reached home as night was falling. Joe parked the van at the curb in front of the Hardys' house. The phone was ringing as they opened the front door. From the living room, Mrs. Hardy called, "That's probably for you, Frank. Callie has been trying to reach you."

Frank raced for the phone and picked it up on the fourth ring.

"Frank, listen," Callie said. "I spoke to Stephanie. She agreed to meet and talk to me. We made an appointment for eight o'clock, at the Starlight Diner on Route Thirty-five. You know the place, don't you?"

"Sure," Frank replied. The Starlight was one of the last old-fashioned diners in the Bayport area.

"I'm a little nervous about going by myself," Callie admitted. "Would you mind coming along?"

"No problem," Frank told her. After some discussion, they agreed that Callie would go alone in her car, so that Stephanie wouldn't be suspicious of anything. The Hardys would go separately and be waiting in the diner parking lot at eight sharp.

The Starlight was shaped like a railroad dining car, with chrome siding and long windows. Joe drove around to the side and parked in a spot with a view of the entrance. The big neon sign over the diner switched back and forth from pink to green, casting wildly colored shadows across the parking lot.

"Do you see Callie?" Joe asked.

"Not yet," Frank replied. "But we're a couple of minutes early. I'm sure she'll—uh-oh. Trouble."

Four teenage boys were walking across the

79

parking lot, headed straight for the van. They all wore angry, determined looks. Gus French, swinging a bicycle chain, was in the lead. The boys on either side of him were holding baseball bats. The fourth, Dino, had a tire iron in his right hand and was bouncing it threateningly against his left palm.

9 Rumble at the Diner

The gang split up as it approached the Hardys' van. Gus and Dino headed toward Joe. The other two moved toward Frank, swinging their bats as they came.

"No ski masks this time," Joe murmured.

"I guess they don't care if we see their faces," Frank replied. "They're probably not planning to leave us in any shape to testify."

"We'd better make a preemptive strike," Joe said. "Look scared. We want to make them overconfident."

"Looking scared shouldn't be hard," Frank said grimly. "If you think it'll help, I'll look totally paralyzed with fear!"

Joe kept his eye on Gus and Dino. Moving

slowly, he reached over and grasped the door handle. Frank was doing the same on his side.

The gang was almost even with the front of the van. An evil grin spread across Gus's face. He drew his arm back to smash Joe's window with the chain.

"One," Joe muttered out of the side of his mouth, "two, *three!*"

Joe swung the door open. It slammed into Gus's chest. He staggered backward and crashed into Dino, who dropped his tire iron with a clatter.

As he reached to turn on the ignition, Joe glanced at Frank. One of the boys on his side had dropped his bat and was holding his hand to his forehead. Frank had a grip on the other guy's bat. He jerked the bat toward him, then, as his opponent tried to pull it back, gave it a hard shove. The small end of the bat caught the boy in the pit of the stomach. He yelled and doubled over.

Joe twisted the key in the ignition. With a throaty rumble, the engine came to life. Gus was on his feet again. He raised his chain for another swing. Joe shifted into reverse and hit the accelerator. The van lurched back a dozen feet, out of reach of the four startled hoods. Joe hit the brakes and flicked on the headlights, then the two quarter-million-candlepower driving lights mounted on the front bumper.

Gus, Dino, and their two buddies raised their hands to shield their eyes from the blinding glare. Joe shifted to low and leaned on the horn as he accelerated. The four Starz jumped out of the way. Something banged against the side of the van as the Hardys sped past. Moments later they were on the street, out of danger.

"Whew!" Joe said. "Next time we run into them, I'd like the odds to be a little more even."

"Joe, we've got to go back!" Frank said urgently. "Callie's car just turned into the diner's parking lot. She doesn't know those creeps are there."

Joe slammed on the brakes and swung the wheel hard to the left. The van lurched into a tight U-turn. The tires squealed loudly. For one sickening moment, Joe was sure the van was going to roll over. Then it leveled off. He aimed the nose at the entrance to the parking lot.

The potent driving lamps lit up the shadowy parking lot, washing out the pink and green from the neon sign. Callie had come to a stop near the back fence. The four Starz were clustered around the same station wagon the Hardys had encountered earlier that day. As the bright beam swept across them, Gus came into sharp focus. Frank could see Gus looking around frantically, then noticing Callie. With an ugly scowl, he ran toward her, his pals only a few steps behind.

Joe steered directly at them. He screeched to a stop, slapped the release button on his seat belt, and threw the door open.

Frank was already outside, ready for battle. "Callie!" he shouted, as Joe joined him shoulder to shoulder. "Get out of here. We'll take care of these guys."

Joe wished he felt as confident as Frank sounded. One of the two bat-wielding boys came running at him, arm raised high. Joe bent over double, then charged. The bat whizzed over his head. Joe grabbed the boy's forearm with both hands and straightened up, then spun on his toes. The gang member's arm wrapped around his own neck. The bat fell from his numb fingers and made a clunking sound on the pavement.

Out of the corner of his eye, Joe could see something move. He dropped to his knees and dove to his left. Dino's tire iron hissed past him and hit Callie's bumper with a loud clang.

Callie jumped out of the car and screamed, "Go away and leave us alone. I just called the police on my cell phone. They'll be here any minute."

Dino blinked and looked over his shoulder at Callie. Joe pushed off as if from the line of scrimmage and hit him solidly, shoulder to midsection. Dino went *whoof!* and fell backward to the ground. Joe met Callie's eye and grinned.

A pair of headlights swung across the parking lot and headed toward them. The car slid to a stop, and both front doors were flung open. Joe turned to face this new, unknown menace.

The first person out of the car was Marlon Masters. He shouted, "Gus, Dino, you guys, back off. The cops are on the way!"

Hedda climbed out from behind the wheel and joined him. "Marlon's right," she said. "This is pointless. You're just asking for trouble."

Dino clambered to his feet, his fists clenched. Joe got ready to defend himself against any blow that came his way. But Dino looked over at Gus, then, seeming to waver, toward Hedda and Marlon.

"Break it off. That's an order," Marlon said. "Scram this minute, or you'll have to deal with me instead of these dorks."

Joe didn't like being called a dork, but he was glad to see that Dino and his buddies were moving away, their shoulders slumped. And why not? Twice they had had two-to-one superiority over Joe and Frank, and twice they had come out on the losing end. Not a great record when you liked to think of yourselves as tough guys.

Marlon trotted over to the gang members. Taking Gus and Dino by the elbows, he walked them to the station wagon, talking in low tones. Then he got in with the four Starz and they drove away. Gus couldn't resist giving Joe a final scowl.

Hedda walked up to Joe, Frank, and Callie. "I'm upset with you," she said. "Upset, and very disappointed. I thought we could work together, but I'm beginning to realize that you like nothing better than to make trouble."

Joe was stung by the scorn in her voice. "All we did was defend ourselves when those creeps jumped us," he said.

"I know why you and your friends came here tonight," Hedda replied. "More spying and prying. You can't deny it, can you? I thought not," she added after Joe and Frank did not reply. "You know, until you started interfering, my work with the Starz was going well. I was beginning to turn them around, to get them off a collision course with the authorities. Now look at how they're behaving."

"You can't keep creeps from acting like creeps," Frank said. "That's the way they are."

Hedda's face grew taut. "Very smart, Frank Hardy," she said. "But I want to tell you this. You and your organization had better get with the program, and do it fast. Otherwise, I am going to see that you have some major headaches."

Not waiting for Frank's response, she turned and stomped off to her car. Moments later she drove away.

"Where are those cops you called?" Joe asked Callie.

Callie gave a shaky laugh. "I don't have a cell phone," she said. "I was bluffing. I knew I had to do something. But I was so scared!"

Joe grinned. "So were we," he told her. "But we came through it okay. Hedda's pretty gutsy, isn't she? I wish she wasn't so down on us."

"What about that girl you were supposed to meet, Callie?" Frank asked. "She didn't show, did she?"

"No, she didn't," Callie replied.

"But the Starz did," Joe pointed out.

"I know what you're thinking," Callie said. "I thought of it, too. But I really don't think Stephanie would help them set a trap for me. I don't know her well, but she doesn't seem like the type who would send someone into such a dangerous situation."

"Then how did Gus and Dino know to come here?" Frank asked. "Not to mention Marlon and Hedda Moon. Coincidence?"

"I don't know," Callie cried. "But I don't believe Stephanie would set me up. Look, I'm going home to call her. Would you mind following me? I'm sure nothing will happen, but . . ."

"No problem," Joe said. "In fact, Frank's planning to ride shotgun with you. Right, Frank?"

"You took the words out of my mouth," Frank said solemnly.

The drive to Callie's house was uneventful. Mrs. Shaw met them at the door. "Some girl named Stephanie has called half a dozen times for you. She sounds very distressed," she said.

Callie gave Joe and Frank a glance, then hurried to the phone in the hall. The conversation that followed was too low for Joe to hear. After a couple of minutes, Callie replaced the receiver and turned to them.

"Dino came over this afternoon to question Stephanie," she reported. "He said he'd seen her talking to me. She got really scared and ended up telling him about our date at the Starlight Diner. After he left, she called to warn me, but I'd already left the house. She wants to get together with me tomorrow. I said yes."

"Are you sure that's such a hot idea?" Frank asked.

"I believe her," Callie insisted. "And I think she needs my help. *Our* help."

Frank looked troubled, but all he said was "Well, okay . . . but be careful. And keep us posted on everything you do."

On the drive home, Joe and Frank talked over the question of Stephanie's role. Was she in on it or was she a victim? If she was a victim, what did she know that the Starz were so determined to keep the Hardys from finding out? Interesting questions, they agreed, but there was no way to answer them without more information.

Back home, they found their parents in the living room. The television was tuned to a program about a new crime bill Congress was considering.

"There's a casserole staying warm for you in the oven," Mrs. Hardy told them. "And a fresh container of chocolate swirl ice cream in the freezer."

Joe grinned. "After listening to some of Chet's ideas for ice-cream flavors, chocolate swirl sounds so bland," he said.

"And so normal," Frank added as the two brothers headed for the kitchen.

Frank served up two portions of tuna noodle casserole while Joe poured two glasses of iced tea, then they sat at the kitchen table to eat. They were halfway through when the phone rang.

"I'll get it," Frank mumbled through a mouthful.

Joe reached the phone first. "Hello?" he said.

"Joe, listen, it's Biff," came a frantic voice. "Somebody just smashed the side window of my mom's car. They got away before I could get a look at them. But they spray-painted a blue star on the windshield. What's going on?"

"I'm not sure, but I can guess," Joe replied. He covered the receiver and relayed Biff's startling news to Frank. Then he said to Biff, "There's nothing you can do tonight, so try not to worry. We'll figure out our next move tomorrow."

"Okay," Biff said. "But in the meantime, what do I tell my mom? She's going to kill me!"

"Just chill . . ." Joe began. But before he could get the rest of the words out of his mouth, he heard a sharp impact outside, followed by a rain of glass onto concrete.

10 Battle in the Dark

Frank ran toward the back door. Joe, who was closer, reached the door first and flung it open. Clearing the steps in one jump, he dashed toward the van. Still on the porch, Frank saw two shadowy figures rising out of the bushes. Both held baseball bats.

"Joe!" Frank shouted. "On your left!"

Joe spun around. Frank jumped up onto the railing of the porch and launched himself at the attacker closer to him. He hit his target at chest height and carried his opponent to the ground. But his opponent twisted as he fell. Frank ended up underneath his assailant, with the boy's bony knee poking Frank under his ribs.

Frank started to push the boy off. He looked up

and saw the butt end of a bat coming straight at him. He twisted his head to the right. The bat hit the ground less than an inch from his ear. Frank clasped his hands together and thrust them up under his attacker's chin. The boy let out a choking sound and fell backward. Frank sprang to his feet, grabbed the bat away from him, and turned to see how Joe was doing.

Joe was doing fine. His opponent was racing down the driveway, leaving his bat on the ground as a trophy. Joe leaned over to pick it up, then decided there was no point in chasing him. I'll know his face next time I see him, he thought to himself.

Let's see what my guy has to say for himself, Frank thought, looking over his shoulder. His opponent seemed to be trying to set a new record for the fifty-meter sprint. He was rounding the corner of the house when the sound of an accelerating car came from the street. He let out a cry of angry despair and ran faster.

Frank looked over at Joe and started laughing. Then he noticed that the side window of the van was broken. The laughter died.

Through clenched teeth, Frank said, "Whatever those worms are up to, we're going to stop them!"

"I'm with you all the way," Joe said. "But the

first thing we'd better do is warn everybody we know to watch out for acts of vandalism tonight. We don't want these guys to give the auto glass shop any more new business tonight."

On their way back to the house, Frank asked, "Your guy—was he one of the ones at the diner?"

Joe shook his head. "Nope. I'm definite on that. How about yours?"

"I don't think so," Frank replied. "Next question—did they have enough time to get here from Biff's house, or are we dealing with more than one platoon?"

Joe gave him a sour smile. " 'Platoon' is a big word for two punks," he said. "But it sure looks like a coordinated assault. And to me that spells Marlon Masters. I doubt if Gus French could manage to mount a coordinated assault on his own shoelaces."

"Don't underestimate him just because he acts like a creep," Frank said. "History is full of efficient creeps."

They went into the house, and Frank dialed Callie's number. She told him that she had put her car in the garage and locked the door. She also promised to turn on the floodlights in the driveway.

Tony Prito was still at Mr. Pizza. His mother, alarmed by Frank's message, said she would be sure to pass it along. In fact, she said, she was going to call Tony the second she and Frank got off the phone.

"I hope we're not like the boy who cried wolf," Frank said to Joe when he hung up.

Joe shrugged. "Too bad if we are. Think how we would feel if someone else's car window got smashed and we could have prevented it from happening."

He took the phone from Frank and dialed the Mortons' number. Chet answered. When Joe told him of the two attacks, his friend sounded alarmed. "Oh, great," he moaned. "If I've got to pay for a broken windshield, it'll take a few weeks' worth of salary. Joe, what's going on?"

"You're in a better place to know than I am," Joe replied. "It's clearly got something to do with Freddy Frost and the people who work there. Do you have something at home that shows everybody's routes? Maybe that'll give us some idea."

"Sure," Chet said. "I'll drop it by tonight. I can't stay, though. I need to be in good shape for work tomorrow."

"Well," Joe said, "if we can't talk tonight, we should sit down tomorrow and hash this whole thing out."

"Hash!" Chet exclaimed. "Of course—hash ice cream! I never thought of that. Why don't you enter it in the contest?"

94

"Look, are you going to meet us tomorrow or not?" Joe demanded. Usually he loved trading quips with his friend, but he was in no mood. "I'm sorry, Chet," he said. "It's been a long day."

"Tell me about it," Chet said. He agreed to meet the Hardys at a luncheonette near the Freddy Frost plant around noon. "And if I have time tonight after I get back from your house," he added, "I'll run up some samples of different flavors of hash ice cream and bring them along tomorrow."

"Don't go to any bother," Joe said as he hung up the phone. "Please don't bother," he added, his mood lightening.

Over breakfast the next morning, Frank studied the chart of Freddy Frost routes. "I have had it up to here with counterpunching," he said. "It's time to seize the upper hand in this case."

"Sounds good," Joe said. He spooned a slice of banana out of his bowl of cereal before adding, "And how will we do that?"

Frank counted on his fingers. "First, we take the van in to have the window replaced. Then we borrow a car. As ordinary as we can find."

"Custom-made for a tail," Joe remarked. "And then?"

"Then we follow Gus French on his ice-cream

route," Frank said. "This whole business started the other day the moment when Chet started driving for Freddy Frost. What we have to do once and for all is find out why."

"Jealousy?" Joe suggested. "Greed and envy? Power?"

"Or all of the above," Frank said in a gloomy voice. "The point is, we don't know. And until we do, this mystery is going to stay as murky as the milk in your cereal."

Joe glanced down, then said, "Do you suppose anybody has made banana-peach-granola ice cream?"

"Don't say it out loud," Frank replied. "If you do, I know who'll try it—and it'll be your fault."

An hour later the Hardys were sitting in the front seat of a light blue economy sedan that belonged to their aunt Gertrude. They were parked thirty yards up the road from the gate to the Freddy Frost plant.

"I wish we'd borrowed something with more power," Frank said. "What'll happen if you have to step on the gas?"

"The car will move in a forward direction," Joe told him. "Look, stop worrying. High-speed chases are illegal in this state, even if you're in a police cruiser with a wailing siren on the roof. And I guarantee that this crate is at least as peppy as a Freddy Frost truck. Speaking of which . . ." As a familiar-looking truck approached the gate, Joe reached forward and turned the key in the ignition.

Frank lifted a pair of lightweight binoculars to his eyes. "That's Gus," he said. "Come on, Joe, let's move!"

Joe rolled his eyes. "Have you ever noticed how slow those guys go?" he demanded. "They must buy those trucks with a special super-low gear. If I don't let him get at least a block-and-a-half lead, we're going to be crawling up his rear bumper!"

For the next forty minutes Joe used all his skill and training to keep Gus's truck in sight without tipping off the Starz second-in-command that he was under surveillance. Sometimes he hung a couple of blocks back, while Frank watched through the binoculars. Other times, he took the risk of passing the stopped truck, then taking a parking slot farther along on Gus's route.

"He's doing a pretty good business for this time of the morning," Frank remarked, during one of these stops. "I'm surprised there are so many people who want to buy an ice cream before lunch."

"They wouldn't send the trucks out if it didn't pay," Joe pointed out. "What surprises me is the route Gus has been taking. Did you notice that he drove right past that playground back there?"

"Uh-huh," Frank said. "And then he parked outside an off-track betting office for a good fifteen minutes. Still, I guess he must know his job. Did you see the way those guys started getting in line even before the truck stopped?"

"Getting their sugar fix before the first race," Joe said. As he did, he glanced in the car's rearview mirror and made a disgusted noise. "Unbelievable! That guy McCay is on our tail again. Do you want me to try ditching him?"

Frank scratched his head. "Why bother?" he said. "We're not doing anything we don't want him to see. Sooner or later, he'll get bored and go home."

Sure enough, the next time Joe checked his mirror, he no longer saw the red car. "Gone," he said to Frank.

"Maybe he's smarter than I thought," Frank replied, checking his watch. "It's nearly time to meet Chet. We can pick up Gus's trail again after lunch."

Chet's ice-cream truck was already parked outside the luncheonette when the Hardys arrived. They found him in a booth at the far end of the restaurant. He had a club sandwich, fries, and a large soda spread out in front of him.

"Hey," Chet said. "I went ahead and ordered. Us working guys don't get unlimited lunch time, you know."

Joe and Frank slid into the seat opposite Chet. When the waiter came over, they both ordered grilled cheese sandwiches and colas.

Frank looked over at Chet and said, "You look worn out. How's it going?"

"Not so hot," Chet admitted. "I'm getting hassled by the Starz members who work at Freddy Frost. You know—making dumb jokes among themselves, bumping into me, sticking out a foot when I walk by carrying a big load of cartons."

"What about your supervisor?" Joe asked. "Hasn't he noticed what they're up to?"

"Sal? Sure, he must have," Chet said. "But he isn't exactly friendly to me, either. I don't know why. We got along fine my first day. And you know, he's not on top of his job. This morning when I got to my first stop, the box in the front of the freezer was empty. Not only that, it was Cherri Cola flavor. That's not even on the menu."

"No wonder," Joe remarked. "It sounds too much like cough syrup."

Chet laughed. "I know. And the really funny thing is that three different people asked me for it this morning. They weren't very happy when I told them I was out of it."

Chet paused, and his face became serious. "I tell you, this job is not turning out the way I thought it would. If things don't get better fast, I'm going to bail out."

Frank twisted his straw in his fingers. Having someone on the inside at Freddy Frost was important to their investigation. If Chet quit now, they might never find out what the Starz were up to. On the other hand, did he and Joe have the right to ask Chet to stay in a situation that seemed to be turning dangerous? He didn't think so.

The grilled cheese sandwiches arrived. Frank took a bite while he debated with himself. At last he decided that it wasn't really his decision to make. Clearing his throat, he told Chet what he'd been thinking.

Chet's face darkened. "Listen, Frank," he said. "I appreciate your concern. But I'm a big boy now. I can make up my own mind. If you think it'll help for me to stay on the job, I will. At least through the weekend. And if I do decide to quit, I'll let you know before I do it. Okay?"

Relieved, Frank said, "Okay."

"And by the way," Chet added, with a mischievous grin. "That's a very drippy cheese sandwich you're holding. It's been oozing down your wrist onto your shirt cuff."

Frank glanced down at his hand. Chet was right. "I'll be right back," he muttered. He slipped out of the booth and went off in search of the washroom. He found it at the back of the luncheonette, just past an alcove that held a pay phone.

After washing his hands, Frank started to open the washroom door. He heard someone say, "Joe and Frank Hardy. That's right—the private eye's two brats."

Frank froze with the door open a couple of inches. Stealthily, he put his eye to the crack. Aaron McCay was standing barely two feet away in the telephone alcove, the receiver to his ear. Luckily, his back was to Frank.

With infinite care, Frank eased the door until it was almost closed. Then he concentrated on listening to McCay's conversation.

"I don't care about that," McCay continued. "Too bad, but we don't have any choice. We've got to eliminate the Hardys and their friends—once and for all. In fact, consider it done."

11 Springing
the Trap

Joe looked up as Frank returned to the booth. "What's with you?" he asked, alarmed. "You look as if you've just seen a ghost."

"This case must be a lot bigger than we thought," Frank replied in a low voice. He slid into his seat. "You're not going to believe what I just heard."

Joe and Chet listened, wide-eyed, as Frank recounted McCay's seeming eagerness to get rid of them.

"So that's why he's been following us," Joe said when Frank finished. "He's setting us up for a hit!"

"Listen, guys," Chet said. "I don't mind mixing it up with a bunch of high-school flunkies like the Starz. But taking on professional gangsters and even murderers is something else. Especially if my sister may end up as one of their targets."

"What now?" Joe asked, turning to Frank.

Frank counted out enough money to cover lunch for him and his brother and put it on the table. "We take him on now," he said. "While he's still just one guy. After that phone call, I noticed that he went back to his seat at the counter. Get ready to leave. The minute he stands up, we follow him outside."

"Bad move," Joe said. "If he's following us, he'll sit there until *we* leave. Besides, for all we know, his friends are on their way here right this minute."

"So what do we do?" Chet demanded.

"How's this for a plan?" Joe said. "We get up now and pretend we're leaving. Lure him outside. Then, as soon as we're out the door, Chet keeps walking toward the parking lot while we hide and wait for him to go by. What do you say?"

"I like it," Frank said. "Chet?"

Chet's answer was to put down the money for his sandwich, fries, and soda, plus an extra dollar tip.

"Let's move," Joe said.

The three stood up and walked toward the exit.

With each step, the sense of tension mounted. Joe found it hard not to look down the counter to the stool where he figured McCay would be sitting. Would he get up to come after them? And what would he do when they confronted him? The answers to those questions were only seconds away, Joe thought, taking a deep breath.

Chet was the first through the doorway. As Joe held the door open, he saw that there were chest-height bushes on either side of the walk. He looked over at Frank and motioned toward them with his head. Frank gave him a quick nod of agreement.

Frank was next through the doorway. The instant he stepped outside, he ducked out of sight behind the bush on the left of the entrance. Joe took the bush on the right and crouched down behind it.

The wait seemed to last forever. Joe began to wonder if his plan was a bust, but the door opened at last. McCay bustled out and stopped on the sidewalk to look in both directions. He seemed nervous.

Joe dashed over and grabbed McCay's right arm, at the pressure point right above the elbow. He gave it just enough of a squeeze to show that he meant business. Frank, meanwhile, had his arm looped through McCay's left arm.

"Time for a casual stroll and a friendly talk," Frank said in a low voice. "That way."

"What are you doing?" McCay demanded. His voice shook. "You boys are making a mistake—a big mistake."

"The mistake isn't ours," Joe told him, guiding him toward the parking lot where Chet was waiting. "It's yours. We don't like it when someone threatens us and our friends."

"Threatens you? Me? That's crazy!" McCay said, his voice rising.

"I couldn't help but overhear your phone call," Frank said. "I heard you tell your friends you were going to have to eliminate us."

McCay heaved a theatrical sigh. "Oh, *that!*" he said. "I can explain that."

"You'd better," Joe said. "And it had better be good."

"Um—would you mind not squeezing my arm that way?" McCay said, looking at Joe from under his bushy eyebrows. "I'm really very ticklish there."

Joe let up the pressure, but kept his hand in place, ready to tighten it if McCay showed the least sign of trying to get away.

"Everything I told you before is true," McCay said. "I'm a freelance writer, and I'm researching a piece on local teens. But what I didn't say is that the focus of the article isn't on hobbies and sports. It's on the recent rise in teen gang activity."

He paused and looked from Frank to Chet to Joe. He seemed to be begging for them to believe him.

"Go on," Frank said. "Get to the part about eliminating us and our friends."

"Bad choice of words," McCay said with a weak smile. "A source told me that you fellows were the leaders of a small but influential gang."

"Who'd be crazy enough to say something like that?" Chet asked. "The Hardys fight crime—they don't commit crime."

"It wouldn't be ethical for me to reveal the identity of a confidential source," McCay told him. "Anyway, when I found out about your detective work, I thought it might be a front to disguise your gang activities. But the more I dug up, the less likely that seemed. So I told my editor that we were going to have to eliminate you and your friends from the article."

Joe looked over at Frank and saw that their thoughts were running along similar lines. McCay's explanation made sense. It was at least as likely as the idea that he was planning to wipe them out. And they had already discovered that he was known as a writer. Joe released McCay's arm and stepped back.

"Sorry for the misunderstanding," McCay said, rubbing his elbow. "Now that our cards are on the table, I think we can help each other out. It's pretty clear that you're investigating the Starz."

"Why do you say that?" Frank asked.

McCay snorted. "Come, come now. I know it, *they* know it. Don't tell me that you yourselves haven't noticed."

"What if we are investigating them?" Joe asked.

"Then I suggest we trade information," McCay said. "I'm sure I have a lot that you don't, but you just might have some facts *I* need. What do you say?"

"We'll think about it," Frank told him.

"You do that," McCay replied. "Do you still have my card? If I'm not in, leave a message for me and I'll get back to you."

Frank took out a slip of paper and scribbled on it. "You can reach us at one of these numbers," he said.

McCay's face brightened. He tucked the paper in his shirt pocket and said, "Thanks, fellows. You made the right decision."

As McCay walked toward his car, Chet said, "So, there's no hit squad after us? Good. I'd better get back to work. Oh, listen—Iola's a little upset with you guys. She feels left out of the investigation."

"Sorry about that," Joe said. "We'll take care of it."

Chet returned to his truck and drove away while Joe and Frank retrieved their car. Frank looked over the sheet outlining Gus's assigned route. "He should be somewhere along Archer Avenue," he reported.

"Roger," Joe replied, pulling into traffic.

Ten minutes later Joe spotted the Freddy Frost truck pulling up to the curb next to a school playground. He stopped half a block away.

Frank chuckled. "It's really something to see how the peewees drop everything when they hear the ice-cream truck coming. Look at that little guy with the soccer ball. I'll bet he couldn't run any faster if he found himself with an open shot at the goal in the last minute of a tied game!"

Joe turned to watch the boy Frank was talking about. He looked to be about eight or nine, with shaggy hair and ears that stuck out. His sweatshirt was muddy and torn at one elbow. He was clutching a dollar bill in his right hand. And Frank was right—he was running as if he had Olympic gold in front of him and a vicious dog on his heels.

The boy stopped short and stared straight ahead. His shoulders slumped. He stuck the dollar bill in his jeans pocket and walked back the way he had come.

"What—" Frank exclaimed. "Gus is driving off!"

Frank was right. The Freddy Frost truck was already at the end of the block. Near the spot where it had been parked, a small crowd of kids milled around. A few of them had ice creams in their hands, but most didn't.

"Pull up there, Joe," Frank said. "There's something here that doesn't make sense."

Joe drove to the middle of the block and parked. He and Frank got out and approached one of the older boys in the crowd.

"Hey, what happened to the ice-cream truck?" Frank asked. "I wanted to get a fudge cone."

The boy wrinkled his nose in disgust. "That dope drove away before we could get over here," he said. "He always does that."

"Yeah," a smaller boy said. "You gotta be standing right here when he comes, or forget it!"

Joe raised his voice. "How many of you were waiting to buy an ice cream when the truck left?"

About a dozen hands went up.

"Tell you what," Frank said. "When we get home, I'm going to call the Freddy Frost company and tell them what's been going on. You guys have as much right to buy an ice cream as anybody, right?"

"Right!" the crowd of kids yelled. They cheered as Frank and Joe got back into their car and drove off.

"Turn west on Washington Street," Frank said after studying the route map. "Gus should be somewhere along there."

He was. The white truck with the colored lights along its roofline was stopped at a busy street corner. At least a dozen people were lined up at the service window. All but one were adults.

"Gus had better not try to drive away from this bunch," Joe said. "Some of them look like the type who might get mean."

"I have a hunch that they'll all get served," Frank said. "Let's wait and see."

Ten minutes later the Freddy Frost was still stopped at the corner, even though there hadn't been a customer in sight for a full minute.

"Maybe he fell asleep at the wheel," Joe said. "Or—nope, there he goes. And here we go."

Two blocks later Gus double-parked in front of a coffee shop, climbed out of the truck, and headed inside.

Joe made a flash decision. "Wait here," he told Frank. "I'm going to search that truck." He got out and ran to the truck before Frank had time to argue him out of the idea.

The inside of the Freddy Frost truck was jammed with equipment. A narrow passage between the two front seats led back into the service area. Joe edged through and paused for one moment to look around him. The machine that made frozen custard was just to the right of the sales window. Below the window was a locked safe with a slot in the top for depositing cash. On the opposite wall was a line of freezers.

Joe lifted the lid of the first freezer. It was full of boxed goodies, each box labeled in large handwritten letters. Most of the lids were open, giving him an appetizing view of the array of cones and ices. He resisted the temptation to take one and moved on to the next freezer.

The inside of the second freezer looked much the same as the first. Joe was about to close the lid when he noticed that a well-used box in the middle was labeled Cherri Cola. Wasn't that the flavor that Chet had mentioned, the one that wasn't even on the menu? he wondered.

Joe lifted the lid, then let out a low whistle. The cardboard carton was half full of cash. A few bills were singles and fives, but most were tens and twenties.

Joe reached into the carton and pulled out a small pad of paper. The pages were perforated halfway along their length, and about a third of the pages already had the lower part torn off. On each of the stubs was scrawled a three-digit number.

"So that's it," Joe said out loud. No wonder

Gus didn't care that much whether he sold any ice-cream cones to kiddies.

He replaced the pad in the carton and closed the freezer, then turned to leave. But as he did, he felt the truck rock to one side. He knew what that meant. Gus had climbed back into the driver's seat. The only way out was past him. Joe was trapped.

12 Taken for a Ride

Joe stood perfectly still, even though he knew that all Gus had to do was turn around to see him. Any noise, any movement might alert Gus that an intruder was in the truck. Yet Joe knew he had to get out of sight—and fast.

Joe looked around, scanning the crowded space for a place to hide. He thought he spotted a gap between the frozen custard machine and the rear wall of the van. Could he possibly squeeze himself into it? He had to take the chance.

Joe lifted his left foot, moved it toward the rear of the truck, and set it down as delicately as if he were walking through a flowerbed full of rare blossoms. Shifting his weight, he took another

113

careful step, then another. He was more than halfway to the niche behind the custard machine when the truck shook from the vibration of the starter motor. The noise of the engine would cover any he made. Joe dashed across the last few feet and flattened himself against the wall.

With a jolt, the Freddy Frost truck started to move. Joe tried to think calmly about his situation. Yes, he was hidden for now. But the next time Gus made a stop and came into the back, he would be bound to spot Joe. And once he knew that Joe had been inside the truck, he would guess the rest. Joe and Frank would lose a precious advantage. No, if possible, Joe had to keep his intrusion a secret.

What if he jumped from the truck the next time it stopped for a traffic light? But the service window was shut. The only ways out were the two sliding doors in the front. Joe couldn't imagine how he could slip out through one of them without being spotted.

Joe took a deep breath. If he couldn't sneak out, he would have to do it another way. At the next stop, he would creep up behind Gus, knock him out, and run. Gus would certainly know that *someone* had been in the truck, but he wouldn't know *who*.

From somewhere behind the truck came the insistent sound of a horn. Joe tried to ignore it.

Then something clicked in his mind. The honking made a pattern: *short-long-long-long*. He knew that. It was Morse code for *J—J* for Joe? he wondered. Yes! Frank was right behind the truck, about to make a move.

Joe braced his arms against the van wall and the side of the custard machine. The sound of the horn was moving up alongside the truck now. Gus leaned on his own horn. Tires squealed as the truck's brakes locked in a panic stop. Joe had been expecting something along those lines. Even so, the shock pitched him forward. His head banged against the metal side of the custard machine.

Dizzy, Joe surged forward toward the front of the truck. Gus was out on the street, shouting and shaking his fist. Frank had leaped out of the blue car, which was in front of the van, blocking its way.

Joe, bent double, slipped out the right-hand door of the Freddy Frost truck and between two parked cars to the sidewalk. Once there, he straightened up and ran out into the street again, as if he were just arriving.

"Hi, Frank," he called. "Any problem?"

Frank shook his head. "Nothing we can't handle," he said.

"Get that crate out of my way, or I'll move it for you!" Gus yelled.

Frank looked over at Joe and said, "Not very original. I heard better back in fourth grade. Didn't you?"

Joe studied Gus's reddening face for a moment. "Uh-huh," he said. "In a minute he'll start calling us names. Then when that doesn't work, he'll probably stamp his foot and tell us we'll be sorry."

"Okay, that's it!" Gus sputtered. "You are going to be sorry!"

Frank gave a satisfied nod. "You called it, Joe," he said. "Come on, let's go, before we fall asleep from boredom."

Joe started toward the blue car, past Gus, who made a gesture as if to grab him. Joe stopped and looked him in the eye. Gus's gaze fell first. Joe walked on, while Gus shouted insults at him.

They drove off, and Frank said, "I hope that comedy was enough to keep him from wondering where you showed up from."

"It was probably enough to keep him chewing nails for the next week," Joe replied. "Or until he realizes that we just cracked this case. Which I think we did." He told Frank about what was inside the Cherri Cola carton.

Frank glanced over at him with a puzzled expression. "So, what's their scam?" he asked.

"They're running a numbers racket out of the Freddy Frost trucks," Joe said. "Don't you see? People bet money on a three-digit number. If their number comes up, they win. If it doesn't, they don't."

"*I* know that," Frank said. "But there's nothing illegal about that. You can play the numbers anyplace that sells lottery tickets."

"Sure, and plenty of people do," Joe replied. "But the lottery commission takes a big cut of the prize and then reports it to the tax authorities. So lots of serious gamblers would rather use a private numbers operation. The payoff is better and you don't have to pay taxes on it. And *that* is very definitely illegal."

"So that's why all those adults were waiting in line for the Freddy Frost truck," Frank said. "Illegal gambling. And the Starz are right in the thick of it. No wonder they wanted to scare Chet out of his job. They were afraid he'd catch on to what they were doing."

"What I'm wondering," Joe said, half to himself, "is whose idea was it? Who's in charge? Not Gus, that's for sure."

"Marlon, do you think?" Frank replied. "He's the only one in that bunch who's got the smarts."

"Maybe," Joe said. "But what about Sal, the foreman at Freddy Frost? He'd be in the best spot to run an operation like this. That would explain why he turned against Chet. And don't forget McCay. There's nothing that says a writer can't be a crime boss in his spare time."

Joe stopped at the next gas station. While he

filled the tank, Frank used a pay phone to call home to see if they had any messages. When Frank returned to the car, he looked puzzled.

"McCay called," he reported. "I called him back. He wanted to pass along something he just learned from one of his sources."

"What?" Joe asked.

Frank scratched his chin. "Well, apparently two gangs in towns near here just signed a peace pact. The Gutfighters and the Gimps."

"I've heard of the Gimps," Joe said.

"You won't hear of them anymore," Frank said. "They changed their name. Now they're the Mad Martians. And the Gutfighters changed their name, too, to the Comets."

"I think I liked Gutfighters better," Joe said. "You didn't say anything to McCay about the numbers racket, did you?"

"Are you kidding?" Frank replied. "As far as I'm concerned, this information-sharing deal is strictly a one-way street, at least until I have a few more reasons to trust him."

At the next corner, Joe said, "Let's go talk to Dad. If the numbers racket is at the center of this case, I think we need to call in a consultant."

They returned home and found Fenton Hardy in his study. He was reading and highlighting a report from a Florida lawyer who sometimes did assignments for him. When Frank tapped at the door, Fenton looked up and said, "Come on in, boys."

Frank and Joe sat on the old leather couch near the wall of bookshelves that held their father's impressive collection of crime literature.

"We've been working on a case at school," Frank began. "And we think we've found a connection to a numbers operation."

"Interesting," Mr. Hardy said, putting down his pen. "And unusual."

"Why's that?" Joe asked.

"Numbers isn't the huge business it was before the government started its own version," Mr. Hardy said. "But that doesn't mean it's a street-corner operation. To make out well, you need to have both brains and deep pockets."

"But you've told us lots of times that in gambling, the guy who runs the game always wins," Frank said.

Mr. Hardy smiled. "And so he does. Look at numbers. The winning number is usually based on something random, such as the amount bet at a particular racetrack. The odds that any given three-digit number will come up are roughly one in nine hundred. If you bet a dollar and you hit, the operator pays you seven hundred and fifty dollars."

"Wait a minute," Joe said. "If the odds are nine hundred to one, but the payoff is seven hundred and fifty to one, that means the operator rakes off about a hundred and fifty dollars for himself. Sounds like a good deal to me."

"Of course it does," Mr. Hardy said. "It's a very good deal. If you have enough people betting, and they spread out their bets, you make out very well indeed—in the long run. But let's say that one day, a popular number like 777 hits. All you took in was a few thousand dollars. But you owe your customers ten thousand, maybe even ten times that. If you have a big organization with lots of resources, you can ride it out. If not, you'd better be prepared to get out of town very fast, go very far, and stay gone for the rest of your life. Which may not be that long."

"Hmm," Frank said. "I see what you mean. It doesn't sound like the kind of racket a gang of high-school students could break into."

"Not without some important adult backing, no," Mr. Hardy replied. "I'm sorry if I've ruined your theory about this case."

"I wouldn't say you've ruined it," Joe said, getting to his feet. "But you've sure given us a lot to think about."

"Frank," Aunt Gertrude said, "you look like someone who could use another piece of my strawberry-rhubarb pie."

Frank looked across the dinner table at Joe and smiled. "No, thanks, Aunt Gertrude," he said, placing his fork on his dessert plate. "It was terrific, though."

As he and Joe were getting up to help clear the table, the doorbell rang.

"You get it," Joe said. "I'll finish up here."

Frank went to the front door and looked through the peephole. Callie was standing on the doorstep, glancing nervously over her shoulder. Frank tugged the door open and said, "Hi. Come on in."

"I would have called," Callie said. "But I figured you'd be home, and I didn't think this should wait."

Frank ushered Callie into the living room, where Joe joined them.

"I just saw Stephanie," Callie told them. "She was too afraid to be seen with me anywhere in Bayport, so we met at the food court of the mall over near Shore Haven."

"What did she tell you?" Joe asked eagerly.

"Well, first of all," Callie said, "the big reason she broke up with Dino is that the Starz were getting involved in some kind of illegal activity. She wasn't sure what, but she knew she didn't like it."

"Just as we suspected," Frank said with a nod.

"There's something else, too," Callie said. "I don't think she meant to tell me this, but it slipped out. It's supposed to be a really deep secret."

"Well?" Joe asked. "What is it?"

Callie twisted her fingers together. "According to Stephanie, the Starz are getting together with a lot of other teen gangs around here. They're going to become a kind of super gang."

"We heard something about gangs just a few hours ago," Frank said. "Two gangs that made peace and then changed their names."

"Did you hear anything about their having one ringleader?" Callie asked.

"No, nothing like that," Joe replied. "Why?"

"Because Stephanie let something slip," Callie said. "When she realized that she'd mentioned the name to me, she got so pale that I was afraid she was about to faint."

"One superleader?" Frank asked. "You mean like Marlon?"

Callie shook her head. "No. Somebody much nastier and more powerful than him. Somebody they know only as the Lunatic."

13 Supergang

"The Lunatic!" Joe exclaimed. "Sounds pretty *crazy* to me."

Frank threw a sofa pillow at him. "This is serious," he said. "Callie, what else did Stephanie tell you?"

Callie shrugged her shoulders. "Nothing, really," she said. "I think she was sorry she'd agreed to meet me. Deep down, she half-wishes she could make up with Dino. But if he ever found out she talked to me about Starz business, he'd never look at her again."

"She doesn't know how lucky that makes her," Joe said.

Frank and Callie pretended not to hear him. "Did she say anything else about this person named the Lunatic?" Frank asked. "Anything at all?"

"Not a word," Callie replied. "I'm telling you, she was scared to death that she'd even mentioned the name to me."

"I guess we know what our next job is," Frank said. "To uncover the real identity of the Lunatic."

"Can't it wait until tomorrow?" Joe pleaded. "This has been a long day, and we still have to do the dishes and finish Aunt Gertrude's strawberry-rhubarb pie."

Gradually Joe became aware that someone was shaking his shoulder. He partly opened his eyes and groggily said, "Wha—?"

"Get up," Frank said. "We have to be at the Coffee Spot by seven-thirty."

"Huh? Why?" Joe managed to say through the fog of sleep.

"We need to talk to Con Riley," Frank explained. "But we don't want him to *know* we need to. So we're going to run into him accidentally while he's having his usual coffee and doughnut before he goes on duty. Get it?"

"Got it," Joe said, throwing the covers back and sitting up. "But I wish he went on duty at ten instead of eight."

The Coffee Spot was located in downtown Bayport, just around the corner from police headquarters. At that hour Joe had no trouble finding a parking place right in front. Through the window, he could see Officer Con Riley at his usual table, leafing through the paper. When the Hardys came in, Riley looked up and nodded to them.

"Rising early, aren't you, lads?" he said. "Not up to anything, I hope."

Joe and Frank got doughnuts and juice at the counter and carried everything over to Riley's table. As Frank and Riley chatted about the latest multimillion-dollar sports contract, Joe kept listening for an angle.

On the drive over, he had agreed with Frank that he would find a way to steer the conversation around to the topic of teen gangs. But how, without being obvious?

Finally jumping into the conversation, Joe said, "Too bad so much money goes to big-time pro sports. What if they used more of it to support local athletics? It would give kids something positive to do, instead of getting involved in gangs and stuff."

Riley raised his eyebrows. "You think so?" he said. "I'm all for more local sports, mind you. But in my experience, the punks who join gangs don't have the sense of hard work and discipline you need to succeed in team sports."

"Still," Frank said, "you have to admit that gangs do attract some kids who could have gone in a better direction."

Riley paused to dunk his doughnut in his coffee and take a bite. Then he said, "I'm no expert. But it seems to me that once gangs reach a certain size and influence, a lot of kids join just for their own safety. They don't see any other choice. And confidentially, I'm afraid we're getting close to that point right here in Bayport and the whole area."

"Really?" Joe said. "I know they're a problem, but I didn't realize they were that big a problem."

"There's a reason for that," Riley said. "I see the statistics every week, so I know. Gang membership around here is climbing fast, but there hasn't been any increase in gang violence. If anything, it's dropped. You'd think the rumble has gone out of style."

"Why?" Frank asked.

Riley shrugged. "A lot of the credit should probably go to an outfit called Teen Peace, run by a woman named Hedda Moon. It has a short-term contract with the town to work with teen gangs. I'm not usually a big fan of do-gooders, but whatever she's doing, it seems to work. Word is, the other towns around here and even the county and state are very impressed by the results. I wouldn't be surprised if they don't pour more money into the program."

"We've got more gang members lately at our school," Joe remarked. "Some of them don't seem so peaceful."

"The Starz, you mean," Riley said. "Yeah. Don't worry, we've been keeping an eye on them. But the word is, they're not such a bad bunch. They're starting to turn in a more positive direction."

Joe choked back the words that rose to his lips. Was operating an illegal numbers game a more positive direction? And what about the intimidation and violence against him, Frank, and their friends? What was so positive about that?

"How's your friend Chet doing?" Riley continued. "The one who's driving a Freddy Frost truck? Any more adventures like the other day?"

"Oh, he's okay," Frank said. "Starting out on a new job's always tough, though. His latest worry is that he doesn't think his boss, Sal Vitello, likes him."

Riley laughed. "Tell him from me that your boss doesn't have to like you, as long as he's fair."

He folded his newspaper and pushed his chair back from the table. "Well, I'm off to the salt mines," he said. "Nice of you guys to drop by.

And whenever you're ready to tell me what's going on between you and the Starz, give me a call."

Riley dropped a tip on the table and left. Joe looked over at Frank. After a moment they both laughed.

"I guess we didn't put anything over on him," Joe said. "He knew we came here looking for him, and he had a pretty good idea why."

"I'm afraid you're right," Frank said. "But did you notice? When I mentioned Sal Vitello, he didn't react at all. I don't think he even knew the name."

"But if Vitello is this mysterious crime boss Callie told us about, you wouldn't expect the police to know him," Joe pointed out.

"The Lunatic . . ." Frank said in a faraway voice. "I wonder. . . ."

"What?" Joe asked.

Frank shook his head. "Think about what Con told us. Gangs are growing fast around here, but they're not battling each other the way you'd expect. Doesn't that sound as if what Callie learned from Stephanie is right? This Lunatic is getting the gangs to join together and become a supergang."

"You think it's Marlon?" Joe asked.

"I don't know," Frank admitted. "Marlon's got the leadership abilities, but I don't see members

128

of other gangs going along with being led by the head of the Starz. There's probably too much bad feeling already built up. Somebody from outside, who doesn't have ties with any particular gang, might have better luck."

"Someone like Sal, you mean," Joe said. "Or—I know this may sound crazy—someone like Aaron McCay. After all, his research for this so-called article has put him in touch with all the different gangs in the area. What if the article is just a cover for the Lunatic's work?"

Frank frowned. "I guess it's possible," he said. "But then why would he have told us about the pact between the Gimps and the Gutfighters?"

Joe grinned. "You mean, the Mad Martians and the—what was it?—the Comets. Maybe he just felt like bragging about his latest success. Or maybe he really *is* a lunatic."

Frank stood up. "I don't believe it," he said. "But we'd better see if we can eliminate him. I doubt if we'll be able to reach him until later, but we can use the computer to dig a little deeper."

The Hardys drove home and went to work.

An hour later Joe straightened up from the computer monitor and said, "So what do we have?"

Frank scanned his notes. "McCay's not married. His driver's license is fairly clean—one ticket for running a stop sign and one for speeding in the last two years. He has half a dozen credit cards, but he carries a big balance on only one of them and his payments are on time. Ditto his utility bills."

"One odd thing—his car was registered new just seven months ago, but there's no record of an auto loan. Did he pay cash? And if he did, where did it come from? Most people don't have that kind of lump sum sitting around."

"Numbers operators do," Joe said. Then he added, "Face it, we don't have anything here to tie McCay to criminal activity. If only—"

The phone rang. Joe picked it up on the first ring.

"What are you doing home?" It was Chet.

"Answering the phone," Joe said, then laughed at his own joke.

"Now *I'm* not in the mood," Chet said. "Listen, remember yesterday, when I told you Iola was feeling left out of the investigation? And you guys promised to find her something to do?"

"Oh, right," Joe said. "I'm sorry, Chet. I forgot. We'll get on it right away."

"But that's just it," Chet said. "Iola went off first thing this morning to check out a lead over at Freddy Frost. I thought she was meeting you there. But if you're home . . ."

Joe felt the first stirring of fear. "I don't know

anything about it, Chet," he said. "What was this lead she was going to check?"

"She wouldn't say," Chet replied. "But she did say she'd be back by nine. Joe. That's more than an hour ago, and she's still not here. Something must have happened to her!"

14 Iola Plays It Cool

Joe told Frank the shocking news that Iola was missing after going off to the Freddy Frost plant.

"We'd better go over to the plant and check it out," Frank said, looking worried. "Can Chet meet us there in fifteen minutes?"

Joe passed on the request, and Chet agreed. As soon as he got off the phone, Joe told Frank, "I think we should bring Callie, too."

"I'll call her," Frank said, reaching for the phone. After a brief exchange, he hung up and said, "Okay. She'll be waiting in front of her house. Let's roll!"

Fifteen minutes later Joe pulled up behind Chet's car, and they got out. Chet hurried over to join them. "Iola's car is parked up near the gate," he blurted. "She must still be inside."

"Okay, here's the plan," Frank said. "We go in together. If Sal is there, Chet will distract him while Joe and I sneak inside and search for Iola."

"And, Callie," Frank continued, "you're our early warning signal. Stay to one side and keep a sharp lookout. If you spot anything that looks like trouble, yell at the top of your lungs."

"I think I can handle that," Callie said. "They'll be able to hear me down at the police station."

The four friends walked along the chain-link fence surrounding the Freddy Frost parking lot. The gate to the driveway was locked, but the smaller sidewalk gate stood ajar. They pushed through it. Frank motioned to Callie to move off to the left. While Chet walked openly toward the loading dock, Joe and Frank sneaked in, using the parked trucks as cover.

Joe grabbed Frank's arm. Sal had just walked out onto the loading platform and seen Chet. The Hardys ducked behind a truck and listened.

"You're here way too early, Morton," Sal called. "I can't let you take out a truck for another half hour."

"Oh, that's okay," Chet replied. "I wanted to get some help from you about our product line. Sometimes kids ask for stuff and don't call it by the name we use. I don't always know what to give them. Here, I'll show you what I mean."

Joe peeped over the hood of the truck. Sal was walking down through the lot to the spot where Chet was standing. His back was to the Hardys. "Now!" Joe whispered. He sprinted between the trucks to the loading dock, then put both palms on the platform and vaulted up. He dashed inside and waited, flat against the inside of the loading-dock door, catching his breath. An instant later Frank ducked through the door.

"I don't think anybody spotted us," Frank said, panting.

Joe took a hasty look around. Just ahead were parallel rows of stainless steel machines. Pipes and plastic tubes linked them to tall insulated tanks along the side walls. A maze of roller belts led from one bank of machines to another. No one was in sight. Nothing moved.

"Take the left aisle," Frank breathed. "I'll go right. Meet me at the back."

Joe nodded. He glanced both ways, then sprinted over to the left aisle and ducked behind a machine that smelled strongly of vanilla. He heard no shouts of discovery, only silence. He was more and more convinced that the plant was empty.

Still keeping a watch to both sides, Joe straightened up and walked toward the far wall. Iola was nowhere in sight. Anger and hopelessness warred in Joe's mind. If anyone had harmed Iola, he would pay them back with whatever it took. But where was she?

Joe noticed four heavy wooden doors set into the back wall at regular intervals. Racks between every two doors held long, thick coats. Joe gave the wall a puzzled look, then muttered to himself, "Oh, sure. At an ice-cream plant, you have to have cold rooms."

Joe was starting to look around for Frank when a spot of color drew his attention. At the base of the machine closest to the back was a scrap of material. Joe hurried over and picked it up. It was a filmy scarf. He was certain he had seen it before, on Iola's shoulders.

A faint noise made him start. He spun around, his hands raised for combat. Frank was hurrying toward him. "She's here somewhere," Joe whispered, holding up the scarf. "See?"

Frank scanned the area. "Joe, look," he said, pointing toward the nearest locker. "The door is wedged shut!"

A triangular piece of wood had been jammed under the handle of the door latch. Joe looked left and right. None of the other locker doors was wedged that way.

"Quick!" Joe said, dashing across to the door. "Iola may be in here!"

Joe grasped the wedge and pulled, but the piece of wood was lodged in place. When he tried to wiggle it, it wouldn't budge. Desperate, he took a step to the side, balanced on one foot, and kicked it with all his might. The wooden wedge tilted sideways. Another kick, and it clattered to the floor.

Frank grabbed the door handle and pulled. The heavy door began to swing open, but too slowly for Joe. The moment the gap was wide enough, he darted inside, then stopped, stunned by the cold. "Iola?" he called into the pitch-black room. "Iola!"

A shaft of light from the doorway penetrated the space and fell on Iola, huddled on the floor, clutching a blanket.

Joe rushed over. "Iola! Are you okay!?"

Frank was beside him, helping him lift a shivering Iola to her feet. Through chattering teeth, she spoke. "Joe? Frank? I was sure no one would come in time."

The two Hardys carried Iola out into the warmth of the plant. Gradually, the color returned to her face. She glanced from Frank to Joe. "Thanks for saving me from my own crazy scheme," she said.

"What happened?" Joe asked.

"I thought I could find out something by searching the plant," Iola said. "So I sneaked in a little while ago. The next thing I knew, somebody threw a blanket over my head and shoved me into this huge freezer. I tried to get out, but the door must have been jammed. I won't tell you how I felt."

"I can imagine," Joe said, putting his arm around her shoulder. "You didn't get a look at whoever did this?"

Iola shook her head. "Sorry. I can't tell you a thing."

"I can tell you one thing," Frank said. "We're going to find them and see that they get what they deserve."

Joe heard a yell from the loading dock.

"That's Callie, warning us," Frank said. "We have to get out of here fast!"

Joe took Iola's left arm and Frank took the right. They started running toward the doors. But before they were even halfway there, the aisle was blocked by a line of grim foes. One, the grimmest of them all, was Marlon Masters.

"So you thought you could frame us," Marlon called. "Make out that we're some kind of crooks. That I'm some kind of crime boss. But we're not sitting still for your dirty tricks."

Joe scanned the area, looking for an escape route. It was then that he noticed, to one side of the Starz, Chet, held firmly by Sal Vitello, and Callie, in the grasp of—Hedda Moon.

"Come on, guys," Marlon yelled. "Grab them!"

The group of Starz started down the aisle. Joe reached over, grasped the handle of a cart stacked with steel milk cans, and gave it a shove. The cart careered ten feet, then scraped to a stop against a machine. The milk cans cascaded to the floor and rolled toward the Starz. By the time they had dodged around them, Joe, Frank, and Iola were almost to the back wall of the factory.

Frank dashed into the freezer locker. When he reemerged, he had two big cardboard cartons in his arms.

"Whatever's in these," he said, gasping, "throw it!"

Joe grabbed a carton and ripped it open. He instantly recognized rows of Freddy Fudgies. Too bad—that was one of his favorite flavors, he thought as he pulled one out. It was frozen as hard as a rock. He launched it in the direction of the Starz. Not waiting to see where it landed or what effect it had, he grabbed another and threw it, too. Next to him, Frank and Iola were doing their part, using Rainbow Ripple cones as their ammunition. From down the aisle came cries of pain and anger as the missiles hit their mark.

Frank shouted, "Hold it. Truce!"

Joe stopped with a Freddy Fudgie in each hand.

"Marlon?" Frank said, taking a step forward. "You think we're trying to frame you and take over the Starz, right?"

"You know it, you creep," Marlon shouted back.

138

"Then who is the Lunatic?" Frank countered. Silence.

"Who made the Gutfighters become the Comets, and the Gimps become the Mad Martians?" Frank continued. "That was the Lunatic's work, wasn't it? And who decided that your name was going to be the Starz?"

"We did," Marlon said, in a voice that now sounded indecisive.

"Oh, sure," Frank said scornfully. "Don't kid me. That was the Lunatic's work, too. And it's the Lunatic who's been trying to frame you, to push you aside and take over the Starz, not us. Haven't you figured it out yet?"

Marlon strode forward, ahead of his paralyzed troops. He stuck out his chin and stared at Frank. "Prove it—right now," he said. "Or I'm going to grind you into a new flavor."

Frank gave a short laugh, then said, "How are you with Romance languages, Marlon? Don't you know what a lunatic is? It's someone who's under the influence of . . ."

Marlon's face changed. In a low voice he said, "The moon." He stood still for a moment. Then he whirled and pointed at Hedda Moon. "You? This is all your doing!"

In the tense silence that followed, the scene looked to Joe like a still photo in an old album. Then Hedda released her grip on Callie and ran toward the loading dock. Joe was next to break

139

the spell. He ran after her. He reached the open air just as Hedda jumped into the driver's seat of the nearest Freddy Frost truck. The engine howled as the truck accelerated toward the closed gate.

Joe reached deep inside himself and found a spare bit of energy. Sprinting as never before, elbows high and knees pumping, he dashed after the truck and leaped up onto the rear bumper. He flattened his body against the back of the truck and braced himself. He knew that at any moment the truck was going to crash into the factory gate.

15 A Wild Ride

As the Freddy Frost truck picked up speed, Joe groped desperately for a handhold. He saw a narrow gap between the top of the rear door and the truck body. He wedged his fingertips into it—just in time. With a lurch, the truck crashed through the gate, then bottomed on its springs as it swerved onto the street.

At the next rough movement, Joe knew he'd be thrown to the pavement. He had to find a better grip, but where? He craned his neck and saw the frame that encircled the roof and held the Freddy Frost lights and sign. How solid was the frame? he wondered. He knew he had no choice—the only way to find out was to try it.

Tightening his left hand into a claw to strengthen his hold on the top of the door, Joe let go with his right hand and reached up as far as he could. His hand touched the front of the frame, but he couldn't quite make it to the top edge. There was no time to hesitate. He crouched slightly, willed all the power into his legs, then leaped.

Joe felt his feet leave the bumper. He shut his eyes, sure he was about to crash to the street. Then his right hand closed over the frame. For several terrifying seconds, he dangled by one arm. Then, with a grateful thought for every chin-up he had ever done, he pulled himself up far enough to grab hold with his left hand, too. Moments later he was hooking a foot over the frame and scrambling onto the roof of the truck.

Joe took a moment to lie flat, catch his breath, and think through the situation. He was much safer now. Unless the truck rolled over, he was not in danger of being thrown off. But safety wasn't the point. The goal was to stop Hedda Moon before anything more happened. And to do that, he needed to be inside the truck, not perched on the roof like it was a tour bus.

Closing his eyes, he tried to imagine the interior as he had seen it when he searched Gus's truck. Along the left wall were the freezers. The plastic service window was in the right wall, about four feet from the rear of the truck. Was there anything directly under it? Joe thought frantically. He only remembered a narrow shelf and a cash box.

Joe tightened his grip as the truck braked and turned left. Then he wiggled over to the right side of the roof and peered over the edge. The service window was directly below him, the top edge only a foot and a half down. But the window was closed. How strong was the plastic? He was about to find out.

Like the trained athlete he was, Joe visualized each aspect of the move he was about to make. Then he took a deep breath, fastened both hands on the wooden framework, and launched himself over the side of the truck. As his body pivoted in space, he jackknifed at the waist and stiffened his legs. His high-tops hit the glass with enormous force, smashing the window.

Joe let go of the roof, tucked one elbow in front of his face for protection, and straightened out. His body followed his feet and legs through the window and into the truck. But as it did, the back of his head banged against the shelf below the window. Joe slumped to the floor, dazed.

The truck swerved one way, then the other. As he rocked back and forth, Joe tried to figure out what was going on. He struggled to his feet and staggered toward the driver's seat. Hedda was swinging the wheel to the left, then the right, slaloming down the center of the street. Horns blared as cars coming the other way dodged out of the truck's path.

"You've ruined everything!" Hedda screamed over her shoulder to Joe. "But they won't catch me. I'll kill both of us first!"

Joe saw through the windshield that they were only a block and a half from an intersection with a busy avenue. It looked as if Hedda might carry out her threat. Joe lunged forward and tried to grab the wheel, but Hedda elbowed him in the stomach. With a scream of tortured metal, the truck sideswiped a fire hydrant. Joe lost his balance and fell forward. His hands hit a switch on the dashboard. A moment later he heard a familiar melody start up. The words rang in his mind even while the truck was speeding toward a deadly crash.

Freddy Frost is such a treat
We bring dessert right to your street

There wasn't a moment to lose. Joe lunged again at the steering wheel. This time he changed the direction of his attack at the last moment. Taken by surprise, Hedda swayed off balance, leaving Joe the opening he was hoping for. He reached forward, grabbed the ignition key, and twisted it to Off. Then, for safety, he pulled out the key and threw it out the window.

The Freddy Frost truck coasted to a stop yards from the crowded intersection. Joe kept a firm grip on Hedda, even while she tried to claw at his face. He was relieved to see three other Freddy Frost trucks and two police cruisers pull up next to him. Frank, Chet, and Sal Vitello ran over to the side of the truck, followed by Con Riley and his partner, Officer Anderson.

Joe handed Hedda over to Riley and Anderson, then stepped down into the street. Frank and Chet crowded around to shake his hand and pound him on the back.

"That was some acrobatic trick you did," Sal said, with an admiring look. "Did you ever think about joining the circus?"

Frank grinned. "Sure he has . . . as a clown!"

Joe grinned back and aimed a punch at Frank's chin—a very slow punch that ended as a tap.

A familiar red car came speeding up and squealed to a stop. Aaron McCay jumped out, a notebook in his hand.

"This is an outrage!" Hedda proclaimed, as Officer Anderson handcuffed her. "You don't have anything against me!"

Sal rolled his eyes. "Oh yeah, lady? How about grand theft auto for a start?"

Anderson and Riley led Hedda to the police car. As Riley opened the back door, she shouted, "I'll have your badges for this!"

"Yes, ma'am," Con Riley replied. "Please watch your head as you get in."

The police car pulled away. Sal watched it go. Then he turned to the Hardys and their friends. "Let's get these trucks back. We still have ice cream to sell today."

At the Freddy Frost plant, Frank was surprised to find Marlon Masters deep in conversation with Callie and Iola. He looked up as Frank and the others came in.

"I think I owe thanks to all of you," Marlon said. "I couldn't understand why all my plans to make the Starz a real community organization kept failing. I blamed you guys. But all along, it was Hedda and her bunch who were playing me for a chump."

Frank looked around. "Where's Gus?" he asked.

"He split about ten seconds after Hedda did," Marlon said with a grim smile. "I'll bet Bayport High will get his transfer papers tomorrow morning."

"Would you fellows please fill me in?" McCay asked plaintively. "What was Hedda Moon after?"

"Maybe that will come out in court," Frank said. "Here's what we figured. She was trying to unite all the gangs in the area. You're the one who put us onto that. But she was also building an official city organization to work with gangs. The more important the gangs became, the more funds and grants she planned to get for her work with gangs, and the more of that money she could funnel to the gangs themselves. And of course, at the same time, the gangs were starting to take over rackets like the numbers game. Pretty neat . . . and it almost worked."

"I feel like such a dope," Sal said. "She talked me into hiring Starz members as a way of helping them go straight. She even convinced me that my man Chet here was a spy who was out to wreck her program."

"He was," Joe said. "In a way."

When the laughter died down, Callie turned to Iola. "What brought you over to the plant this morning?" she asked. "And who put you in the freezer?"

Iola shook her head. "I never saw who it was," she said. "As for why I came, I wanted to help. And from what Chet said, I was sure that the solution to the mystery was here. I was right, too."

"I can guess who attacked you," Sal offered.

"The only guy here that early, except for me, was Gus. And I know *I* didn't do it."

"He called me to say that you guys were over here trying to frame the Starz," Marlon said. "He must have called and warned Hedda, too."

Frank glanced down at the desk and noticed the flavor contest folder. "Sal? Did your boss pick a winner in the contest?" he asked.

"Yeah, he did," Sal said with a grin. "There were some really strange entries, but the winner was strawberry-rhubarb-pie flavor. Submitted by someone named Gertrude Hardy."

"Aunt Gertrude!" Frank and Joe shouted together. "All right!"

"You guys stay here," Sal said. "This calls for a celebration. I'll be right back with a round of Freddy Frost Berry Nice Swirls for everybody— on the house."

He hurried off toward the coolers.

"Celebration? Yes! That's it," Chet exclaimed. "The perfect thing for a festive occasion. Champagne ice cream with caviar topping!"

Everyone stared at Chet in silence.

"Hey, that was a joke," Chet said, grinning. "You don't really think I'd want to put fish eggs on ice cream, do you?"

The group stared at Chet for a long moment. The laughter that exploded gave Chet his answer.

"Chet, good buddy," Frank said as Sal returned. "One of these days we're going to make you eat one of your concoctions."

"No, thanks," Chet said with a grimace. "I think I'll stick with the Freddy Frost favorites," he added as he took a large spoonful of his Berry Nice Swirl with a cherry on top.